Viva

México

Kerri Shute Tarpey

Copyright © 2016

All rights reserved.

ISBN:-10: 1523959932
ISBN-13: 978-1523959938

CHOOSE TO BE THE PERSON YOU TRULY ARE

Viva México

Table of Contents

Acknowledgments	
The Way Home	5
Papi	17
Absinthe Dance Club	41
Maria	49
The Plan	63
Pulling it Together	73
The War	89
The Captives	99
The Mayor	113
Frankie	125
Pedro	139
Maximo	149
Bad News	157
Confessions	167
Games	175
Decisions	191
Without a Plan	201
About the Author	219

ACKNOWLEDGMENTS

To the Mexican-American woman who screamed wildly at a town hall meeting somewhere in Arizona (or perhaps Texas) without regard for the news camera, you were my motivation for researching this topic. Your passion, desperation, and dedication to your family compelled me to write about why so many people have left México. I truly hope that you have found peace.

Mark Veilleux, thank you for believing in me.

Shelley Baglino, I am forever grateful to you for the hours of editing you selflessly contributed to this project, and I just can't thank you enough for your encouragement and friendship.

To my pre-reader friends: George Spies, Lou Prosperi, Sharon Beebe, Emily Holmes and Colby Hewitt! Your comments and contributions have been invaluable. Thank you.

Love to all.

1

The Way Home

Miguel stood out among the other riders on the Greyhound bus. He was youthful, standing tall in his military fatigues like an unbroken man. Picking the only row of seats that remained empty, he slid over to the dusty window, closed his tired eyes and rested his head on his rolled up jacket against the glass. He prayed that no one would sit next to him. Sleep found him quickly. Much of the trip back to the town of Del Guardo, and his father, passed undisturbed.

When Miguel awakened, his thoughts were of the road. He wondered where he was. The land was parched. The brown tips of green scrub bushes proved their longing for relief. A bony, sand colored dog ambled along the shoulder, its tongue wagging longer than its motionless tail. Miguel recognized these things as life in Arizona on the border of México.

As Del Guardo became visible in the distance, Miguel's stomach began to gnaw at him. He cast his vision to the horizon to escape the tightness of the bus which had begun to close in on him. Memories of how he ended up living in Del Guardo flooded his thoughts. He recalled the day the cartel attacked his hometown of Esperanza, México when he was thirteen years old.

***

Miguel had been flirting with Gabriella as they played far too long in the crowded outdoor market, the heart of the town of *Esperanza*. His mother was waiting for the groceries at home. He knew that the best produce sold first and that he should have made his selection long ago. His mother would be disappointed.

The market was a colorful, bustling place to while away the morning. Merchants displayed their wares along the sidewalk. Boys selling newspapers, soft drinks and sticky treats were jumbled in with beautiful handmade blankets and pottery. The streets had been alive with the sound of a mariachi band playing at the street corner. The festive atmosphere disguised the ugliness and corruption that had taken root in the town.

The local gangs, a part of the much larger drug cartel, had been extorting money from these merchants. The cartels took a substantial bite out of everyone's income. If a merchant did not comply, citizens vanished. It was rumored that these missing people were shot and left in shallow graves to drown in their own blood. Innocent workers had been murdered in the streets in order to motivate their bosses to pay up, which they always did. Politicians and police had been coerced, some with rewards, some with threats; there had been no help for the townspeople.

Miguel was alert, hearing the SUVs round the bend before anyone saw them. He grabbed Gabriella's arm hard and pulled her into a narrow alley. Miguel pressed himself against her as though this might keep her safe. Their breath was heavy as they waited. Rifle shots and screams filled the air. Eyes darting in panic,

Gabriella pulled him closer. She lifted her face to press against his and squeezed her eyes shut. Miguel kissed her forehead and then her lips. In that moment of sweet comfort, he was struck on the head and fell to the ground, unconscious.

Miguel became aware of Gabriella screaming. She was struggling, but it was easy for the cartelista to twist her slender arm behind her back as he tore at her skirt. Miguel tried to reach out to her, but he faded out unable to help.

When he awoke next, Miguel found himself being dragged by the shirt into the street and dropped onto a pile with other boys. Many had already been tied up, but limp and appearing unconscious, no one bothered to bind him. He watched Gabriella dragged into the street as well. She was tossed onto a pile of women who sat on the ground crying and clutching each other. Their eyes were those of wild dogs. Having heard stories of what would happen next, panic filled them.

The cartelistas stole what they wanted from the town. Taking cash, food and supplies, they shot men in cold blood while sons looked on from the pile. Women were raped and beaten bloody. Some fell to the ground as though dead; many were dead.

The townspeople had heard that the cartelistas always beheaded at least one woman in the street for all the living to see. The uproar diminished as the men tired from the work of terror. Some could be heard laughing, between gulps of bottled water, as they stood in small groups by their vehicles sharing stories of their victims' struggles. What was stolen had been loaded into trucks, but they didn't leave. Several began to stride around the pile of women who kicked and struggled in vain to move away.

The cartelistas circled and provoked the women and girls by prodding them with the butts of their guns as they passed by. One man reached down and snatched a woman by her dress. When it ripped, he grabbed hold of her hair and pulled. She leaned back and screamed, swinging at the hand gripping her hair. She looked like a lobster that flips its tail and splays its claws to avoid the confinement of the small bag while the fisherman smirks at its futile attempt to live.

The beheading didn't happen quickly. They made it last. The men did not register any emotion. It was part of their job, like taking the head off of a chicken is for a butcher; it was perfunctory.

Having harassed the desperate woman for a time, the cartelista bent her head forward as she sat, hands tied behind, her legs crossed at the feet. The first whack of the foot-long dull blade didn't kill her. Her body popped upward and fell over into the dirt. The second strike did not kill her. The man sawed at her neck while another plodded over with an axe and swung, quickly shearing off her head. It spun aside and landed on the first man's foot. He jumped away shouting, "Hey, be careful. You ruined my new boots." He bent over and lifted the slippery, heavy head in the air for all to see.

Quiet sobs and muffled moans were heard from the boys. The women and girls were silent in their shock. No one struggled any more. Dropping the severed head, the executioners walked back to begin loading the children.

Those that wouldn't fit in the vehicles, were left tied in the street. Their turn would come another day. There was a sudden outburst of wailing as the trucks sped away. Some screamed as though madness had consumed them. Hands still bound, they struggled to right themselves. Nothing would ever seem beautiful again.

Soon after the trucks had gone, Miguel cleared his head enough for complete thoughts to form. He looked for Gabriella, but she was nowhere to be found. He needed to run. He needed to get away from the marketplace and find his family.

***

The Greyhound slowed to a stop. A tear rolled down Miguel's cheek, forming a path through the salt and dust. He quickly wiped the tear and braced himself for the final leg of his trip back to his father's farm.

Miguel made his way from the bus station to a nearby bar. As he walked, he noticed a man in tattered clothes leaning on one elbow against a wall, protecting a bottle inside a brown bag. A beggar's jar rested by his feet. Young boys in over-sized, low-hanging pants cruised up and down the middle of the road with a confident, yet spastic, gait. Passing cars honked their horns, but the boys didn't deviate. Teen-age girls, wearing only enough clothing to cover a small child, perched on stoops. They gestured with claw-length painted fingernails as they gabbed, snapping their gum while continually scanning the streets.

Most of these kids should be in school, Miguel thought. From the looks of it, they think they already know everything they need to know in this life.

Many of the buildings built a hundred years before, maintained a sweet charm despite a facade that had become faded and worn. The shabby gas station looked out of place next to the new, brightly colored nail and hair salons. A barbershop and its candy cane pole had passed the test of time. The newsstand and a shoeshine boy seemed to have escaped from the past. The town appeared flashy and cheap, yet its stone walls and stucco houses provided hints of the allure it held in a different time, in a more wholesome culture.

Miguel needed to collect his thoughts before facing his father. He sat down in a chair at an outdoor table that was much too rickety for his heavy frame. Without asking, a waitress placed a plastic cup of water on the table and asked, "What else?" Miguel ordered a beer from the tap.

Head lowered with fatigue, Miguel smoothed the plastic checkered tablecloth with his hand and thought back to the table in his childhood home in Esperanza. It was his grandmother's table. He remembered how she would scold him for leaning back in the chair while he boyishly smirked at Gabriella who sat opposite him. Slipping his foot out of a tattered shoe, Miguel would stretch his toes out in search of her leg. He was unable to reach her without leaning back, so Gabriella would slowly extend her leg out to find his. She would blush as he slid his foot as far up her leg as he could. She wouldn't move away, and they would both smile. Miguel had always felt alive when he was with her.

The waitress disrupted Miguel's memories when she set the beer down in front of him. The glass was scratched and white with frost. His mouth watered as he brought it to his lips. These surroundings were familiar, the people were not. Across the street, three well-dressed men approached two others. They shook hands and disappeared inside a restaurant. People watched them with discreet, nervous glances. Miguel observed people moving past the old man and his beggar's jar as though he didn't exist. The vacant expression on the man's face suggested that perhaps he wasn't there, not his mind anyway.

Miguel paid the bill. Standing up with a heave, he left. He could have called for a cab but, as much as he wanted to see his father, he was reluctant to go to the farm. He'd make his way on foot.

On the main street, he bent onto one knee in front of the old beggar and waited to be noticed. The man's watery eyes reluctantly came into focus and Miguel said while pointing at the jar, "I used to have one of those. Are you a soldier, sir?"

The man cleared cobwebs from his vocal cords, "I am."

"Thank you for your service. But, it's time to go home, sir. Do you think you could find your way home?"

The man was slow to answer, but nodded and said, "I might. It's hard to remember the way. I might be able to if the war is finally over."

"I understand. It's over, Soldier. It's time to make your way home. I'll bet your family misses you." Placing twenty dollars into the man's hand as he shook it, Miguel whispered, "God bless America."

He set out toward his father's farm but faltered quickly. The day was hot and his duffle bag seeming much heavier than before. The cry of an animal summoned his attention. He stopped, looking down to see a mangy grey cat carving figure eights around his legs. So thin, she looked almost flat. She purred as he bent down and poured water from a plastic bottle into his palm. Once satisfied, the grateful cat turned her head, concentrating on a spot in the brush. Miguel realized that she must be a mother. He followed her gaze, and then followed her, needing to see something beautiful. Her babies were just that. Maybe three weeks old, the four tiny kittens pushed themselves around aimlessly bumping each other. They missed Mama. She laid herself amongst them and began to clean herself as they nursed. "I know how you feel," Miguel whispered as he stroked them with a finger, and his broken heart broke again. The comfort of a mother's love was something he barely remembered.

Back on the road, Miguel's pace slowed, his mind to drifting back to his journey from México to the US, shortly after the cartel's brutal raid on his hometown.

***

Miguel's parents and younger brother, Juan Carlos, had hastily packed what they could; mostly water and food along with their heavy hearts. They could afford to pay a coyote to guide them to a crossing point on the Rio Grande to *el Norte,* the United States, a place they both respected and resented. From there the family would be on their own.

It was harder and hotter than they had worried it would be, and it was lonelier. It was so powerfully lonely to walk away from everyone they knew and loved, everything they once held dear. With their destination unknown and survival unlikely, their grief was palpable.

Miguel had slept for most of the first two days as the group moved from truck, to car, to truck again. Nauseous and sometimes gagging, slightly concussed from the blow to his head in the alley, he might have thrown up had he eaten, but he had not.

The driver came to a dusty stop in the middle of nowhere. His frown and furrowed brow warned that something was wrong. He unloaded the family's meager possessions as they prepared themselves. "Your small boy is sick," the coyote said. "He will burn with the Fever before long. He needs a hospital. I have seen his look many times before."

"He's fine," Papi said. "*Gracias amigo*, but it's a chance I have to take."

The coyote placed his own bottled water with their modest pile of belongings, then handed Papi a roll of thick parchment. "This will be your most valued possession," he explained, "Use it to funnel water should God bless you with a rainstorm. Make shade for the boy otherwise." Turning his back to them, he drove away without another glance. The small family became immediately overwhelmed by isolation. And silence.

Moving slowly across the hot, dry land, it was still difficult for Miguel to think. At times he would fall to his knees and drop prone onto the burning sand. He needed to sleep, to heal the damage to his head. They would rest, his father assured him, if they found shade. Papi curled the parchment over Miguel's head, hoping the shade would ease his son's headache. Miguel held onto his father's shirt as he plodded along.

After the second day of walking, with the heat traveling relentlessly along, their pace slowed to a shuffle. Fever had begun to drain Juan Carlos's strength. Papi wrapped Juan's arms about his neck and lifted the boy. "I love you, Juan Carlos. Papi loves you.

Don't be afraid. Papi loves you." The weaker Juan became, the heavier his little body seemed. Papi suddenly collapsed, placing Juan in the narrow shade cast by a small pine shrub.

Miguel listened to his parents as they planned the next move. "Already, he is not even conscious. I should have listened to the coyote," Papi said in a hoarse whisper. "I can't carry him anymore. My boy is going to die in this God forsaken desert. We will die with him while we wait. I don't know what to do."

The food rations were depleted. Mama passed the last of the water to Miguel. "Mama, you didn't drink."

"I don't need it. You are young. Drink," she said. Miguel noticed that her breath came in short puffs like she was panting.

"You and Papi are going to walk together. I am going to stay back with Juan and continue on later."

Papi's voice had evaporated in the heat leaving him only the scorched, hoarse sounds of wailing. Too withered to even make tears, Papi turned his face to the heavens with folded hands and prayed. Miguel had begun to realize that Papi was saying goodbye to Mama and Juan Carlos, offering the only aid he could in the form of prayer. Miguel fell into his Mama's lap. Mother would never leave Juan. Once Miguel understood that, he wondered how he could ever leave them behind. But, he wanted to live.

That night, Papi prepared a shallow hole for the family to sleep in, pushing the sand back onto them to serve as a blanket. The frosty the night air forced them to huddle closely, shivering until daybreak in the grave like depression Papi had created. They slept during the short temperate breaks between the two extremes of night and day.

Mama was slow to awaken. "Promise me, Papi, that you will bring Miguel to America. Promise me." Papi nodded his head and she turned to Miguel saying, "I love you my brave boy. Be strong."

"You're going to come along, right Mama?" Miguel asked.

"My love will always be with you even when I can't be. God bless you, *mi hijo.*"

Mama tried to call out one last "I love you." as Papi and Miguel slowly walked away. Her strength depleted and her throat dry, her voice didn't reach them. She brought her hand to touch Juan's sweet, sleeping face and closed her eyes awaiting the relief death would bring.

Miguel's fingers once again found his father's shirt tail that had served as his guide and held it tightly. His eyes, squinting against the sun's blazing light, could see the hazy white cotton shirt, soiled with silt and sweat, just ahead of him. The knot in pit of his stomach warned him that he would most likely never see his mother or brother again, but he couldn't feel anything. He couldn't understand it. He could only feel the sun searing his face, the sting of the rash that had formed under his arms and on his neck, and the blisters that bit his toes and heels with every step.

In his mind's eye Miguel could picture his mother and brother, lying there in the sand, but it seemed like an awful dream. Bringing them back to life in his thoughts, he could see Mother's soft brown curls bouncing as her smiling face approached him with a kiss on his cheek, pulling him into a hug. He could remember Juan Carlos as he dashed into the house for meal time. It seemed that Juan had always been running.

The memory of Juan's boundless energy made Miguel smile, causing his lips to crack and bleed. He tried to lick them with his tongue, which was stiff and thick inside his mouth. Involuntarily Miguel swallowed air and dust setting off a gag reflex, and suddenly he was thrust from his pleasant daydream and once again boiling in the desert heat, behind his father's sweat-stained shirt.

***

Miguel had stumbled close to the street while lost in grief as an eighteen-wheeler roared past. The wind from its wake pushed and turned him as he once again became oriented to his surroundings. He folded onto his knees and remained there on the barren ground.

A pickup truck slowed as it approached and then stopped, the driver waiting to be noticed. "Quiet!" he called to the four growling dogs in the flat bed. Miguel slowly struggled to his feet as the man spoke.

"Hey, Soldier, you okay? Need a lift?" Without looking at the man, Miguel nodded with obvious relief. The driver stepped out of the truck, walked to Miguel and began to guide him toward the side door.

"Your dogs don't seem too friendly," Miguel said.

"They're not. They'll eat you dead or alive," he laughed. "That's the way I want them to be. I make sure they're always a bit hungry, just in case. No one is coming onto my property without my say so." Miguel glanced back to the flatbed as though the dogs might confirm their owner's convictions. "On your way home? Your father is waiting for you."

Miguel asked, "Do you know me?"

"I do. I remember you from when you first came here to Del Guardo from México. I am a friend of your father's. My name is Ben. We take care of each other. He has been looking forward to this day for four years."

2

Papi

Miguel rushed his steps, dropped his bag and crashed onto his father with an audible sob, burying his face in his father's neck and shoulder. It had been four tiresome years since he last felt the strength and comfort of his father's grip. Their embrace was long and powerful. Thumping each other's back, silently shedding tears of joy and relief, the two men slowly rocked. Finally able to release each other, Papi turned to Ben, "*Gracias, mi amigo*. I appreciate your help."

"No problem."

"Can you come in and visit a while?"

"Enjoy your boy. I need to get these crazy dogs home before they eat someone," Ben said with an earnest shake of Papi's hand, he left.

Miguel and Papi walked arm in arm to the house. Miguel asked, "Is he serious? Will his dogs really attack someone?"

"Never doubt it. Those animals are dangerous."

Wordlessly moving into the dining room, Miguel pulled back a chair and sat. It was not his grandmother's chair or his grandmother's table, nor was she or mother there to instruct him to wash up before sitting down. There was no one to kiss his forehead or to tell Miguel with a proud grin how lucky Gabriella was that her handsome grandson loved her. He'd left those treasures behind in his childhood with all things good. Papi gradually portioned whiskey into two small glasses and slid one toward his son.

"Welcome home. It's so good to see you. How are you?" Miguel's head nodded barely meeting the gentle gaze falling from his father's worn face. He was too full of emotion to speak.

Miguel didn't have the words to say how he felt. What he longed to say should not be said by grown men. He wanted to be held tightly by his Papi. Returning to the farm had overwhelmed him with grief. This place is where he had learned to live without his mother and brother after having left them behind in the desert. He mourned the loss of his childhood in this house, the loss of Gabriella, and his home.

The American military had provided an escape from Miguel's past and any reminders of it. It gave him a way to release some of his anger. But, he had learned the hard way that taking a life of any kind, for any reason, even the life of an enemy, echoes in a man's soul as much as the pain of the loss resonates forever among those who grieve. Miguel had replaced a heart full of grief with a heart full of guilt. Living with remorse and feeling like a murderer weighed heavily on him. He thought himself to be no better than the cartelistas back in México.

Miguel knew he would ache with sorrow as he learned to live with his past, with what war had done to him and what he had done in war. The relief a bullet would bring on the battlefield of the Afghanistan was no longer something for which he could hope. He had no place else to run. Back at the farm, he would have to find the courage to face it all.

His father reached a calloused, tentative hand across the table and touched his son. "You are my greatest joy. I couldn't be more proud of you." Miguel flashed his eyes toward his father without actually seeing his face. Even looking into his father's eyes felt like it required courage.

"I'm tired Papi. I am so tired. I need sleep." Miguel said.

"And a shower," his father added with a chuckle, "You probably need that more than sleep."

Miguel smiled and allowed himself laugh for a moment. He looked around the room, "It is good to be here with you, Papi." Shaking his head he added, "But, this farm, it cannot replace Esperanza, Del Guardo will never be home to me."

***

Morning arrived without his consent. Miguel rolled around in the bed until it was too hot to sleep, and finally he gave in to meet the day. Papi had served a breakfast of eggs, ham and toast and left it on the table hours before. This was not the breakfast his mother would have put out for him, but he was glad to have it and ate it cold. Adding ice to the coffee, Miguel headed outside to the shady porch.

Miguel scanned the horizon and watched barely visible waves of heat beginning to lift themselves into the atmosphere. He thought back to his first day at the farm.

The mesas and buttes at the horizon with their flat tops and steep sides had been no substitute for the green majestic mountains of México which could be seen in every view. These were uninviting barriers resembling giant soldiers that had died but hadn't fallen.

Back then, Miguel and Papi had agreed that the old farmhouse might have been built by an assembly of neighbors rather than experienced craftsmen. The front corner had dropped a bit lower than the rest of the house giving it a contorted stature. The roof shingles had pulled away in places, and the windows were boarded up, but Miguel didn't mind. He was weary from being half-starved on the Arizona streets, tired of not knowing where his next meal would come from, and fed up with wondering which dirty corner he was going to sleep in each night. Crowded soup kitchens and handouts left him hungry and unsatisfied. Angry words from indignant strangers had disheartened him.

"We have a farm back home in México. It's beautiful," he once told one man who stopped to put a few quarters in their beggar's jar.

"Why don't you go back to it?" the man had said. Miguel recalled wanting to throw the quarters back at him, but his empty belly had prevented it.

He remembered thinking that he wished somehow he could show the people of el Norte, show all the Americans, that Mexicans were not different. "We are like you. We love our family and friends, our God, our country. We love just like you do. What scares you also scares us."

Miguel wished he could have told them of the horrible losses he had suffered at the hands of bad men; the same men who sell these Americans their drugs. He yearned for his mother and his brother. The fate of Gabriella and his friends worried him endlessly. He longed to hear the easy laughter of the Mexican people. No matter how much his people had or lacked, they had laughed and loved and cared for one another.

He missed his home, the marketplace, its noise, its wild colors and grand festivals. Miguel's mouth watered at the thought of his mother's fresh, warm corn tortillas.

The farm offered him a bed, food to eat, and a place to grow in safety. He was pleased, but he could tell that Papi was not. He seemed angry all the time. Papi had steered clear of the gangs of Esperanza and the drug life back in México, making a good living with the farm. Mama taught at Miguel's school which helped the family too. But, to avoid starving on the Arizona streets, Papi had made a bitter deal with the cartel in order to secure the farm.

Papi's nephew, Santino, at the tender age of eighteen had moved up in the local cartel culture, running his own gang. His group was a special kind of cruel. It had been Santino's gangs that had raided their village. These gangs had caused Papi to lose his home, his beautiful wife and son. He was now forced to beg a favor from the same murderous monster. Papi had managed to escape the raids on his hometown, but asking for help meant he would forever be in debt to Santino and his gang.

As a young boy, Santino enjoyed *la comida*, the lunch feast, almost every Sunday afternoon at Papi's home. Papi was like a father teaching Santino many essential things about life, like the importance of God and family. He addressed the things Santino's own father would have taught him if he had lived.

Santino had played games with Miguel and Gabriella. He was older but was never able to win. It was vital for boys to learn well and prove themselves as strong and capable as they changed from teenagers to men. Santino struggled, becoming angry and impatient. Eventually, as Miguel and Gabriella were busy falling in love, Santino found other places to be and other ways to feel potent. That is what the gangs had to offer; they offered power and money. Santino had found something he was skilled at; brutality.

Santino turned Papi's desperation into an opportunity to advance his position in the cartel by acquiring the farm where he could grow his business, just across the border of México. Santino was eager to prove himself. He would move product and people in and out of *Los Estados Unidos,* the United States, while Papi oversaw the operation and absorbed the risk. Papi struck this bargain in order to survive, but after realizing the horror of Santino's trafficking human beings as well as drugs, he wished he had died instead.

Papi knew that being associated with a human trafficker and drug dealer was all the provocation the American government needed to imprison or deport him. Every day he worried about being arrested and feared for Miguel's future. Ashamed, he prayed daily for God's forgiveness, keeping the ugly truth from Miguel and swearing that he would stop Santino if he ever could.

On the rare occasion when drug traffickers were imprisoned in México, they were treated like royalty. None lacked privileges like phones or television. Food could be delivered from restaurants on request; conjugal visits were frequent. In sharp contrast, there was no relief from Mexican connections in Arizona prisons. It was hard time spent in the heat of the desert in brutal conditions.

Miguel's father felt as if he had sold his soul, and any hope of happiness with it, in order to save the only son he had left from the streets to a place where he could at least hope to build a future.

Papi and Miguel never discussed the past, as if not speaking it aloud would somehow erase history, and they might wake up from a bad dream. Miguel felt as though he had lost his father to anger and bitterness. His pain and loneliness matured with him until he hated the farm and *el Norte*, too.

Paying dearly for the documents needed for Miguel to start school, both pretended all was well. The United States teemed with possibilities. It was overflowing with opportunity. But, those opportunities and possibilities were not within the reach of the illegally immigrated. People accepted Miguel and Papi, as they were hard-working and stayed out of trouble, but many were cruel.

At school, the kids called Miguel harsh names, pushing him around at recess in the schoolyard or on the long walk home. There were fistfights at first when the other kids said his English wasn't good enough or his clothes were not "cool" enough. Miguel felt that the children of the US cared about all the wrong things.

At home in México, every boy strived to be the best and the strongest but when they finally could make that claim, they were humble. Everyone knew who "the best" were and being the best, earned respect. Children worked hard and patiently to become superior. They didn't achieve success by putting someone else down. Being the greatest had nothing to do with the clothes a person wore. It was a hard earned glory. Something American bullies would never know.

***

Miguel could smell the barn from where he sat on the porch and noticed his father pushing a wheelbarrow full of horse manure and wood shavings. Watching Papi work for a few moments, he thought about how proud he had always been of his father. He wondered why he had never said this to Papi. Miguel's recollection of Papi from childhood was of a stern man, strong and capable, a man who always worked hard to take care of his family and friends. Papi looked much older now, but Miguel could see he was still the same strong man, and he felt proud.

"Don't you have someone who can clean those stalls for you?" Miguel said as he approached.

"I do," Papi answered. "But, I like to do it. It's only the two horses, so it doesn't take long."

Entering the barn, Miguel noticed that it was constructed of cedar wood and looked newly built. The floors were clean, level and covered with thick rubber. There were four stalls on each side, housing only the two horses which stood across from each other.

Papi introduced his favorite horse first: a quarter horse standing seventeen hands with deep brown coat, ebony mane and matching tail, "This barrel-chested beast is Brown Bear. He's deaf, but he's an excellent horse. We've been together since about the time you left. And, this pretty girl is Buttercup. All sixteen hands of her are as lovable as she looks. She's been with me about two years. She's a dressage horse, but she's coming around to tail riding. She's getting used to the place." Buttercup bent her head so he could scratch her ears. "I thought we'd go out for a ride today."

"Sure, Papi. A ride sounds good. The horses are wonderful—really great. It's been a long time since I rode. I'm glad Buttercup is agreeable."

"She's sweet, but I wouldn't pull any crap. She is as unforgiving of carelessness as any woman ever was." Papi laughed and Buttercup stomped one foot as though confirming Papi's sentiments. "You'll be just fine."

It was hot day, but a refreshing breeze supplied some relief. Miguel found Buttercup to be smart and willing. He began to relax as she carried him along the broad trail. Riding again felt good. And, it was a joy for Miguel to hear his father talk about the farm with such ease and contentment as they rode along. The farm had been an ugly place for Miguel as a young man, with the unappealing purpose of moving illegal substances and sex slaves for an equally unsavory man. But, his own father's designs revealed a more appealing landscape, a place for nurturing and celebrating life.

Papi rambled on about the "gift" of arid soil because it was easier to manage pests that might otherwise get out of control. "We can add water with technology and irrigations systems," he said, "but those unlucky folks who suffer from flooding just have to watch all their hard work be swallowed up." He chuckled and shook his head.

Papi told Miguel about some of the local folks who he was encouraging to experiment with crops on their farm for new markets. "It's more challenging than you would think to commercialize crops that typically grow in the wild. Nature balances itself in ways that she does not reveal. Like the best magician, Mother Nature does not easily give up her tricks. How the Guayule seed tumbles and rolls across the desert floor as though guided home by a compass to finally take root in the perfect setting leaves me mystified."

"I'm not sure that every seed finds a home," Miguel offered. "Maybe it's just that we don't notice how many times life begins in nature only to be lost to unfavorable conditions. If one plant yields one seed per season which takes root, yet another plant yields a thousand seeds but only one survives… which is the better plant?"

Papi scratched his head and pondered his son's question, but left it unanswered. "The locals study what the perfect conditions appear to be and attempt to reproduce them here on the farm, but it doesn't always work. They are having good luck with a few plants like aloe, but it is all-for-naught with others. It's nice to have these people around to chat with; I've learned plenty from them."

The two men passed a cluster of needleless scrub pines, "Who knows what caused all of these to die off," Papi said. "The bare skeletons tell the tale of once having basked in the warmth and glory of God's good graces. They fought a hard fight to prosper, and they won for a short and glorious time."

Miguel said, "We all are called to God in the end."

"They look like an army of bold, brave warriors standing there. I see a monument to the souls of my Mexican ancestors." Papi said. "The men of México are fighting this same hard fight to persevere in spite of impossible conditions every day."

Miguel said, "The irony is that at one time, it is likely that our ancestors did stand right there doing battle, back when the Spanish owned this land."

"That's why I leave them there for now, like the ghosts of old friends," Papi said.

"So are you going to be an organic farmer now or something Papi?"

His father's mood became tense, and Miguel immediately was sorry that he had asked. "No, Miguel. I am not. I have liberty on this part of the farm, the Northern part, to do what I want, but the more fertile areas to the South are governed by Santino." Miguel watched his father's face and thought that just saying Santino's name was causing him pain. For the first time, the gap in conversation felt awkward. Finally, Papi changed the topic. "We have a plane now. It's for spraying God-knows-what on the cotton," he chuckled. "Only the cotton grows where we spray. All other plant life is devastated, but I swear the insects are getting bigger. It's like they are feeding off of the stuff."

More soberly, he forced himself to add, "Santino traffics people through that side of the farm. The kids, dear God, the kids," Papi shook his head as though trying to erase images from his memory. "They are of no use in the club or at parties because of the

Frankenstein scar they wear after being gutted like fish for one of their kidneys. I try to keep them here as cooks or just get them off the heavy work, but I don't have much control.

And, I don't know where Santino finds the foremen, but they are soulless brutes who inject much of Santino's profits directly into their arms. They are usually rapists, too. I don't even want to imagine what night time is like down at the workers' camp." Immense sadness poured out of Papi's expression as he spoke. "Ignacio is the newest foreman and the worst one yet. He's been here a couple of months. I swear, I am gonna shoot him myself one of these days." That possibility turned Miguel's stomach, while confirming that things were as bad as had Papi described. Papi had never been the kind of man who resorted to violence. He had been the type who no one tested on the matter.

"The croppers are quality, hard working people though. Many come back year after year, and I have gotten to know them. Good stock. Some are from our village. I go down to the South side occasionally just to hear about old friends and see if there is any news from home. Your grandmother lives at the church now. She is one of the deacons."

"I'm glad to know she's safe," Miguel said. "I am grateful and relieved. I miss her. What a gutsy old girl she is; a real survivor. Is Padre Cayo still head priest?"

Papi lowered his head a bit, tipping the brim of his cowboy hat down as well, and Miguel sensed that his father was once again uncomfortable answering his questions. "Padre Cayo was replaced a long while back. He was cooperative with the cartel, of course, but not like the new head priest. I don't know where Cayo is living, but he is still around. Your Grandmother stays in touch with him."

Miguel's heart begged to learn Gabriella's fate, but he knew not to ask for fear that hearing her story might ruin him. If there was good news, Papi would have brought it up by now. Miguel decided it was better to pace himself.

"We can ride down to the cotton part of the farm tomorrow. I'm enjoying today too much to go. Are you getting hungry? I asked Cookie to make us a roast beef with garlic mashed potatoes and lots of gravy for tonight. The meat will be our cows, you know. We keep a few dozen now. There's no money in it, but we eat well."

"You are becoming very Americanized, Papi, which may not be a bad thing. I have gotten very used to American food, too."

***

The following morning over breakfast, Papi broke the news to Miguel that Santino had asked to meet with Miguel. He would have to travel back to México soon. Miguel had expected this as Santino would consider Miguel in debt to the gangs as well as Papi, but it was a devastating blow nonetheless to hear the words spoken. He felt sure that Santino would insist that Miguel work for him.

"Maybe I can make a stop at the church to see *Abuela*," Miguel tried to sound pleasant.

"I wouldn't advise it," Papi began slowly.

"Why not, Papi? Wouldn't she be happy to see me?"

"Padre Cayo's replacement is what they call "The Executioner." A pretty scary man."

"What does that mean, Papi?"

"It means," Papi began but hesitated. Saying it out loud was hard for him, "that he is the one who removes the kids' organs. He makes it some kind of sick religious ritual."

Miguel's features twisted in disgust, "I'm not hungry now, Papi." he pushed his plate away.

"Take a break and come back to it. You're going to need your strength for the long ride today."

***

The horses perked up in the paddock when they saw Papi and Miguel coming. "Watch this. Another step or two and they'll start acting up. I don't know how they sense when we have apples for them, but they know."

It was easy for Miguel to see how much these horses loved Papi, but it was even clearer that Papi loved and respected them as well. Both horses seemed excited about riding the trail again today. While Miguel brushed her flank, Buttercup stomped her foot and turned her head to look back at Miguel as though asking what was taking so long. Brown Bear slowly pulled the saddle blanket off of its resting place on the stall door and held it in his teeth. His powerful head gave it a playful shake while he waited for Papi to finish brushing.

Papi rode alone most days, so having a companion would be a treat for both him and the horses. With Miguel's sore muscles burning from yesterday's ride, they mounted, picking up the trail to the South this time.

This side of the farm seemed dustier. Papi pulled his bandana over his mouth and nose, shaping his face into a strange expression. His nose flattened, the skin around his eyes stretched downward and his cheekbones pushed out. He motioned for Miguel to do the same.

"It's not so much the dust as it is the chemical spray that we use to annihilate every other living thing that's not cotton."

Miguel did as instructed, "I hope this look suits me better than it suits you."

"Doubt it." They both broke into a laugh. "Your lungs and brain will thank you though."

The occasional rusted-out car bumped along the dusty, narrow road filled with countless people. Arms and heads were pressed against the front and rear windows, legs and bare feet jutting out the open side windows. Again, finding themselves chuckling at the absurdity of the scene, Miguel and Papi moved off the road into the scrub brush giving them space to pass.

"Today is payday," Papi said. "The workers who don't live here have an easier time if they come in groups, but a man with a car has many friends around here. Most will be back here by 4 a.m. for work tomorrow, but they need that check today, so they endure that absurd ride on their only day off.

These migrant workers earn just enough money to keep their stubborn hearts beating, but most remember when their heart pounded with pride. I remember it too. The pride of being Mexican was the life's blood in our veins." Miguel wondered if it was regret this time or anger that that choked Papi as he force himself to continue. "America will always be the friend who kept them alive in their time of need, but she is only a cheap substitute for their true love. They wait to go home again."

The horses startled and snorted, clearly ill at ease. Papi didn't have much to say and looked more like a hunter now than a farmer, wide eyes scanning the terrain. This change in demeanor left Miguel feeling less conversational, and he turned his attention to the landscape too.

Brown Bear suddenly startled, attempting to walk in any direction other than forward. Papi drew his pistol, whispering a few calming words to his old friend, "Easy boy. Easy. We'll get 'em this time." He kicked Brown Bear into a canter, riding a quarter mile, Buttercup following behind. Just beyond a bend, the foreman's truck was pulled off the road. Papi rode to the far side of the truck where Ignacio stood shouting, the butt end of his gun poised to strike.

A young woman, a migrant worker, crouched on the ground with her arms raised high to protect her head. The foreman's pants were unfastened and hanging from his knees. Holding her by the hair on the top of her head, he was forcing her mouth toward his erection. Her eyes were shut as tight has her lips and she was snorting breath through flared nostrils as she cried.

Papi wordlessly aimed the pistol at the foreman's heart as he suddenly looked up. Ignacio released the woman and clumsily stepped back while gripping his pants in one hand, his gun in the other. Papi changed his sights and fired one shot, ripping a hole through foreman's groin.

Instantly, the foreman dropped his gun and collapsed to a seated position, looking down at what was left of his manhood. His shocked expression changed to defeat as he sat there, legs spread in a pool of his own blood, aware that in a few short moments he would bleed out from this wound. Papi stretched a little taller in his saddle as he watched the foreman deciding what to do with his last few breaths. "I warned you last time, Ignacio, I warned you!" Papi shouted. Ignacio began to sob, his blood-soaked hands covering his eyes until he finally toppled forward, landing with his head between his legs. With only his own boots for company, Ignacio's tarnished soul freed itself from his useless form.

Brown Bear took on a look of boredom as Papi dismounted and draped the reins on his neck. He turned and scuffed a few steps away to find something to munch on. While Miguel looked on, Papi asked the woman if she was hurt and she showed him what looked to be a broken arm and a swollen, blackened eye. It was obvious that she needed to get to the hospital. Papi assured Miguel that Brown Bear would make his way back to the house and directed Miguel to just let Buttercup follow. Miguel wore a pensive expression but nodded in agreement.

Pulling a fallen scrub pine over next to the foreman to block the body from sight, Papi explained that he was going to drive Ignacio's truck to Ben's house to pick up his dogs. Their dinner was ready. He would then deliver the woman to the hospital and return the truck later, leaving it next to where the foreman lay beside the road. Ben would bring him home. When the body was found, it would look like a coyote attack.

***

Miguel couldn't let go of a panicked feeling on the ride home alone. This place felt foreign and untamed. He wondered if anyone had witnessed what had happened. He really wanted to talk to his father. He thought of that poor woman heading off to the hospital.

Miguel's first memory of America had been of a hospital waiting room. Unconscious upon arrival, Miguel had slept sprawling on a couple chairs for two days in the waiting area of the emergency room.

A stranger had spotted Papi at a distance from the main road and had driven across the desert sand to collect him. Papi had pointed his hand in the direction where Miguel lay dying. "My son. Please. Help me," he begged through peeling, sunburned lips. He had left Miguel a mile or so back when he had first begun to hear the roar of moving vehicles. The sound of civilization had given Papi hope and a direction to follow with renewed energy, knowing that the journey's end was near. With all the stamina he had left, he begged the driver to rescue Miguel, having promised Miguel that he would come back for him. The driver was reluctant at first, glancing at his watch in frustration. But, two had gone back by truck to rescue Miguel, who lay unconscious in the dirt where his father had left him.

First the man wetted Miguel's lips and mouth as best as he could. Papi wept openly as the stranger fed sips of water to him. "*Gracias a Dios, gracias a Dios*," Papi mumbled. He sat on the ground beside Miguel, resting in the shade cast by the truck. Overcome with emotion and exhaustion, Papi could barely speak to express his gratitude for this stranger's kindness.

Papi had heard frightening stories of rude unwelcoming Americans. He had been warned to be wary. Sometimes, after completing the long journey across the border, Mexicans had been shot. It was hard for Papi to imagine. He hoped, after meeting this kind stranger, that perhaps Americans and Mexicans might be similar with respect to the value of life and how to treat those in need.

Once inside the emergency room, that hope had faded away. The nurse had unsympathetically asked Papi a few questions—his name, why he was at the hospital and what medications he was taking. She took blood pressure and temperature readings, handed him four bottles of water with instructions that they should drink slowly; one sip at a time over the next hour. Only then could he attempt to eat the applesauce and pudding she had given him. Then more water she had said. She flashed a bright light in Papi's eyes and then Miguel's to observe pupil dilation. She looked for yellowing which might indicate liver failure. She had handed Papi one thin blanket, walking quickly away.

Papi had explained to Miguel that it had been almost impossible to hold a bottle of water in his hand and be told to sip it slowly. But, Papi had known that digestion would take its time to begin again, so he had filled his mouth with cool, clean water one swallow at a time. Papi had slept sitting up until space cleared next to him, and then he too had lain over a second seat next to Miguel. This is the way they had remained for two days. It had become clear that no one was going to admit them or examine them. They had no insurance, no identification and competition for medical attention continued to arrive in the emergency room.

Gunshot wounds were a priority, stabbing wounds and car crash victims were treated quickly, too. If an insurance card was produced, expectant mothers were admitted right away. If not, the baby was delivered in the dirty, crowded emergency waiting room.

Miguel smiled to himself as he recalled his father's description of a gum-snapping woman wearing three inch heels and a yellow wig, who had been accompanied a man and his painful erection that lasted longer than three hours. "It was hard to tell which was more annoying," Papi had said.

Only one person had been admitted before sitting down. He had the Fever. The Fever, as it was called in México, was the same one that had stolen his brother's strength while crossing the desert.

The two things known about this illness were that it was contagious enough to affect everyone in the room in no time, and it was almost always fatal. Miguel and his father had not realized that the Fever had been showing up this far north of the border.

The druggies had been grouped together under police supervision off to one side of the emergency room. Miguel recalled that there had been many addicts. They clogged up the emergency waiting room with the simple hope that detailed descriptions of excruciating pain and aches would convince the doctor to prescribe pain killers. The nurses had known many of the addicts by name.

Each had seemed believable until he or she became impatient and started screaming, ranting and making violent threats. It had been wise to make these individuals wait until their addictions became apparent as a result of their outrageous behavior. Then the police officers would simply escort the offender out of the building and wait until another one began to bluster. Each had performed the same routine, yet seemed to think that they were being original. Other people, barely alive because of whatever they had injected or snorted, were eventually treated.

Lots of people had passed through that emergency room during those two days. Everyone had been a priority, that is, everyone except the illegals. The illegals, who had just survived the border crossing, yearned for water, food and rest. If more than that was needed, they might die of it right there in the hospital because they weren't getting any attention; not without an insurance card.

Miguel could still form vague memories from the end of those two days. He remembered feeling compassion for these people. He wished he could have helped somehow, but at the time he could barely stand or stay awake. Papi had been alert, engaging in conversation with others who were waiting, especially with Mexicans who might be able to advise him of what to do next.

One man had stood up and walked over to Papi, handing him his blanket. A nurse had followed him with her eyes as she talked on a phone squeezed between her ear and shoulder. As he exited the door, the nurse had placed her pencil down, shuffling through a stack of papers. Reading his name on the top of one, she had turned and fed it through a paper shredder. He and his problems had never existed.

***

On the ride back to the house, Miguel was glad to have the company of Papi's horse. At times Brown Bear would stop to eat something. When Miguel allowed Buttercup to trot or canter, praying that nothing spooked her, Brown Bear would overtake them and be their guide for a short stretch. Feeling strange to be led by the beast, Miguel wondered if the clever boy could unsaddle himself too when they arrived back at the barn.

Two days of riding found Miguel sore and stiff. After he unsaddled the horses, one of the workers rubbed them down, fed and watered them. Miguel made his way to the house, ran a hot bath and soaked his tired muscles. There would be plenty of time before his father returned.

***

Papi had left the woman at the door of the ER, knowing it was best not to get involved in these things. He met Ben, waiting at the side of the road where they had agreed, on the way back. It had been a long day, and both men were anxious to put it behind them. With Ben following, Papi drove back to the cotton side of the farm to drop off Ignacio's truck. As they rounded the bend, they were startled to see the police chief's car waiting by the foreman's body.

Papi was shaken. Police showing up on this farm lay so far outside the realm of possibility that he hadn't considered it. He hadn't prepared a story explaining why he was driving Ignacio's truck. Fumbling for his pistol, he quickly wiped his fingerprints off of it, and pushed it under his seat. The Chief pointed at the truck and then to a spot near him, meaning Papi should park the truck there. Ben parked too, but waited in his truck.

The Chief of Police was a large, intimidating man. He carried wide, heavy shoulders on his six-foot frame. Papi was familiar with the Chief, but wasn't fond of him. A blind eye was a convenient possession for lawmen around here. The Chief used his more skillfully than his weapon.

The local police had adopted the Mexican custom of *mordida*, a "little bite" or tip for services rendered, but the Chief was also on the take, so right and wrong only mattered based on where the profit would lie. He was always looking for a payoff, but he also enjoyed hurting people. His relationship with Santino was mutually profitable.

When questioned, Papi admitted that he was the owner of the land and agreed that the half-eaten man did look like his foreman, Ignacio. He shook his head sadly for effect, adding that it was a shame and that he would notify the man's family. Chief Ortiz asked if the truck Papi was driving was his own. Sensing that the chief already knew the answer to that question, Papi said that it was not. While the officer impatiently waited for the rest of the answer, Papi explained that it was actually the foreman's truck.

"How'd you come to be driving it?" the chief asked.

"I came down here today on horseback and found one of my workers had broken her arm," Papi explained. "Foreman here said he wouldn't be needing his truck, so I could use it to take the poor woman to the hospital. I was returning it just now. If you don't mind, I better see how things went today without a foremen supervising. Excuse me."

Chief Ortiz stepped directly into Papi's way. "I do mind. I mind very much. I am on your farm trying to figure out what happened to this innocent man today. He was your man, and you're disrespecting me and him by acting as if I am holding you up. You're acting like men get half-eaten every day. This may be a normal occurrence where you *cholos* come from, but here in the good old US of A it doesn't happen. Now, what do you suppose your foreman was doing so far down this road without a truck? How do you suppose he ended up behind this bush and out of sight?"

"I can't suppose anything. I didn't know him well," Papi stated flatly, "He's only been here for a few months." The Chief continued to stare at Papi, until it had become clear that he was waiting for more than conversation. "He could have been doing anything. Maybe he's a bird watcher."

Papi's sarcasm was exactly the disrespect the chief had been waiting for. "You know, *Cholo*," the chief put his face in front of Papi's and growled, "I overlook the bulk of what happens down this way. I don't ask a lot of questions that maybe I should be asking. What do you think, *Cholo*? Maybe I should take a look around with you. I think I'll begin by taking a peek to see what it is that you are hiding underneath the seat of that truck."

Papi, standing five foot seven, was outmatched by three inches and fifty pounds, but he stood his ground, fists clenched, barely even blinking his narrowed eyes, "You're gonna need a warrant to search that truck," he said almost foaming at the mouth.

Chief Ortiz shoved his chest into Papi and bounced off him, stepping back with a surprised expression. Chief threw himself at Papi again, pushing him with both hands, and this time Papi faltered. "Did you just charge at me, *Cholo*? Who do you think you are, coming at me like that?"

Papi said, "My name is Salvador Garces, try to remember it. Remember this also, while you're at it, you never know when there's a camera rolling… Chief."

The Chief's eyes flitted around as he tried to spot the offending camera. He located Ben holding his cell phone just above the dashboard. Ben's eyes doubled in size as the enraged chief headed for his truck. He fumbled with the screen while stealing glances at his new, invading enemy.

"Any closer and my buddy is gonna hit send. The internet is forever. The truth is much harder to deny once people can see for themselves. By the way, have you informed Santino about this yet?" Papi asked.

The Chief stopped in his tracks. "You think I am afraid of your fucking video? Or Santino? Or you?" he said while storming back to Papi, punching him in the face. Papi stumbled and let himself fall to the ground, hoping that from the ground, he would no longer be a target.

"You better watch yourself, fucking immigrant, before I have you sent back to where you came from. Let Santino deal with you himself, *Cholo*." He wound up to kick Papi as the sound of an approaching vehicle caught their attention. The coroner had arrived. Papi collapsed with relief. The chief quickly backed away from Papi, turning to greet the new arrival. Papi picked himself up and returned to the truck. Both he and Ben set out, continuing down the road to the nerve center of the South side, Ignacio's office, and the bunk house for workers.

***

"At least now I know why you ride a deaf horse, Papi," Miguel said as he entered the kitchen, sitting down to slide his boots on. "Did Brown Bear go deaf from you shooting bullets over his head?"

"That is a very real possibility." Papi was busy scrubbing his hands at the sink. "He is a good horse. He could tell that something was bad a quarter mile away, but he can't hear anything. Buttercup didn't react the same way—just Brown Bear. I am lucky to have him. He gets pissed off about things, same as me.

"How do you know he can't hear?" Miguel teased. "Maybe Brown Bear just ignores you." Miguel sat down at the table and asked, "What are you doing over there?"

"I'm just being extra careful."

"What do you mean, Papi? You look like you're making dinner." Miguel sauntered across the room to examine the ingredients Papi had stacked beside him on the counter. "Vinegar, lemon, olive oil and sugar. Yuk." Standing next to his father, he could see his father's reddened, swollen cheek. "Papi, what happened to you?"

"A present from the Chief of Police. He gave me a hard time when I went back to drop the truck off."

Miguel went to the freezer and prepared a bag of ice. "Here, Papi. Put this on your face."

"Hold on. I have to remove the gun shot residue on my fingers. In case there is more trouble and my fingers plead guilty for me."

"What do you mean?"

"The vinegar cleans, the lemon is acidic, the oil and sugar exfoliate."

"I am relieved that it's not my dinner. So, the foreman's done that before? Ignacio has raped the women here?"

"He has. I caught him once and beat him up a bit. Some of the women have come to me asking for help since then, but without proof, there hasn't much I could do. He has been pretty physical with the croppers, too. I tried to handle it, but it didn't help much or for long. He was just an ass."

"Do you think that's the end of it? Will there be more trouble with the chief?" Miguel asked.

"I don't know, Miguel. I've been thinking about it all day. The police don't come around here. Santino makes sure of it. I don't understand why the Chief was here. Someone had to have called him."

Miguel asked, "Do you think whoever called them saw us out there?"

"I don't know. I am worried about it though," Papi admitted. "The chief is so dishonest, it's usually better for him to simply take the bribes when it comes to Santino's territory. One dead Mexican is not something he would worry about unless Santino told him to. Ignacio had a sidekick. Maybe he has something to do with getting the police here. Maybe he called them to keep me from shooting him as well." Papi's amused expression showed that he liked the sound of that. "I don't think Santino put Ignacio on this farm randomly. I didn't know that for sure until now. Santino has been watching us very closely. I think I can safely assume that Ignacio's sidekick made a phone call to Santino, and Santino sent the police. Perhaps he is applying pressure from his side to remind us that he is able to reach us anywhere."

"Well, my time is up then," Miguel said. "I had better get down to México and see what Santino wants to talk to me about before he makes life too uncomfortable for both of us."

***

Miguel was miserable at the thought of seeing Santino. He prepared his last minute essentials for the flight while Papi waited by the car. Papi was always ready early, but this time Miguel thought, as he pulled back to curtain to check, that Papi was avoiding him by standing out there pacing around. Communication was not one of Papi's many gifts. Miguel wondered which of them was more nervous about this trip.

A duffle bag slung on his shoulder, Miguel heaved a heavy sigh and headed out to join Papi. Noticing a siren wailing in the distance as he turned the lock on the door, he took it as an omen, a foreshadowing of the coming day. He couldn't recall ever hearing that haunting shrill sound so close to home. The sound grew louder until the piercing cry pressed towards them; they both stopped to listen.

Anxiety powerfully gripped Miguel as the blue lights appeared atop a cloud of dust, and the police car came to a halt, blocking the driveway. The chief, presenting a smug expression, was at the wheel. Papi, still bearing the swollen bruise from his last encounter with the chief, put his hands in the air, stepping away from the car.

"No, Papi, no," Miguel pleaded without knowing for what. "Please, NO!" he begged as though God himself might intervene.

"Salvador Garces, you are under arrest," Chief thrust his knee into Papi's thigh causing Papi to cry out in pain as he fell and knelt on the ground. "You have the right to remain silent…" Pressing his boot into Papi's back, Chief pushed him to the ground. He held Papi's face to the dirt with his shin as he slowly cuffed Papi's wrists.

"Save your tears, you have a big day ahead of you." He called out to Miguel while yanking Papi back to his feet. Miguel hadn't even realized that tears were streaming down his own face. His heart was breaking for his father.

"I'll come get you, Papi. I'll post your bail."

"No. You won't. Not today. Your father will be waiting for you when you get back."

3

Absinthe Dance Club

Miguel entered Absinthe, Santino's dance club, following behind two of Santino's escorts, who had met him at International Airport in Chihuahua, México. The club hadn't opened for the evening yet. At first, the dim lighting made it hard to see beyond his own feet. The escorts pointed Miguel toward the bar and stepped away to talk to women with whom they were obviously familiar, giving Miguel a chance to orient himself in the dark room. The dancers' poles rising from the bar in front of him were marred by smudges of residue and fingerprints from the previous evening's entertainment. The bartender tipped his chin in Miguel's direction, but Miguel waved him and the drink he was offering away.

Miguel had heard stories about Absinthe when he was young, but he had never seen it. It was rumored to be the best dance club anywhere. Absinthe's allure drew young people from miles around; international visitors came too. Dancing and music was only part of the appeal. The real draw was that any drug known to man was available in that club. There were no cameras and police were paid not to visit there, unless they were off duty. The club offered strippers, hookers and strong alcohol, too. Absinthe was the place to party in northern México.

Miguel was surprised by the impressive the two-story building. Inside the main area, tables covered with white cloth were set and ready for diners. A large, three-sided bar made of white smoked-glass filled the center of the room, and an area for a band to perform was tucked off in the far corner behind the dance floor. He could see the closed doors of several rooms used for card games or private parties off the main area. Through the spacious back doorway lay a covered patio with strings of small white lights lining the perimeter and a tall rock waterfall with a pool of water in front. There were high-top tables for gathering and another large area for dancing, all bordered by palm trees and decorative flowering shrubs.

The second floor staircase was cordoned off by a thick rope. Most of the second floor was open loft space, mostly visible from below. There were pool tables and dart boards and couches for relaxed viewing of the many televisions. Miguel remembered the stories of small private rooms available for drug use or working girls to rent. He imagined that those were still here, located behind all that furniture, out of sight. Drunks who had managed to pair up and were in need of a private space could rent a home-away-from-home for forty pesos.

The more experienced girls moved slowly and deliberately past Miguel, their high heel shoes clicking on the floor. Others slipped away, clearly hoping not to be noticed. Miguel assumed these girls were new.

A pretty teen-aged girl with long, brown hair barely hidden under a baseball cap carried a large bucket of ice to the bar. It appeared to be heavy, but she handled it comfortably. She turned her back to Miguel, dumping the contents into a freezer. He couldn't help but notice how shapely she was. He was reminded of Gabriella when he last saw her.

Turning around, the girl walked to the dishwasher, tucked under the bar in front of Miguel. She glanced up at him from under the baseball cap and immediately directed her eyes away. He was not sure she had seen him, but he saw Gabriella's face.

"Excuse me," he said.

She looked up at him but continued unloading dishes.

"Um… Can I have a beer?"

Without a word, she popped the top off a bottle and reached to set it on the bar. Miguel touched her hand. She snapped her hand away and wiped it on her jeans, looking startled.

"Who is your mother? What is her name?" Miguel asked far too abruptly.

"Gabriella," she uttered in a meek voice.

"And, your father?"

"Santino," She motioned toward the open door where Santino stood glaring.

Miguel looked back toward the girl, who was already moving away from him, and returned to focus on Santino. Miguel tried to mask his fear, but he knew was failing. His stomach turned sour at the sight of Santino, who approached slowly and made no effort to shake his hand or embrace him. He motioned Miguel to a small table with two seats where they settled in.

"We don't greet like family anymore?" Miguel glanced back in the direction the girl had gone.

"I see that you have met my daughter, Maria." Santino said coldly.

"I have. She is very beautiful. She looks just like Gabriella did as a girl."

"Gabriella is her mother," Santino said casually and paused. He stared at Miguel's face, eager for his reaction.

"Is she your wife? Did you marry Gabriella?" Miguel managed to utter.

The question seemed to make Santino momentarily uncomfortable. Clearly, he hadn't expected it. He sniffed his nose and darted his eyes around the club without really focusing on anything. "She lives with me." Finally pleased with himself for having struck a blow to Miguel, he crossed his legs, sitting back with a grin of satisfaction.

Miguel kept his gaze on the floor while chewing his lip. He knew that Gabriella would never choose to live with such a vile man. He tried not to show the pain it caused him to know that Gabriella was not loved. He fumed at the thought of Santino forcing himself on Gabriella. But, he was relieved to learn that she was still alive.

Miguel had to work up the courage to ask Santino if Gabriella was a hostage. The answer seemed obvious, but couldn't afford to make assumptions. He had to pose the question. He would hate the painful answer, but needed to ask. "Is she your prisoner?" Miguel's lip almost curled with tension as the foul words formed in his mouth. Santino didn't answer. "Are you taking some kind of revenge on me? Why did you have to have Gabriella?" The two men locked eyes. Growing impatient, Miguel pounded his fist on the table. He heard the familiar sound of springs tensioning as metal scraped on metal. Several of Santino's guards had cocked their weapons. Miguel fought to compose himself.

Santino waved the guards away and changed the subject. "You are well, I can see. You have been bold fighting for el Norte, I have been told. It has hardened you. I see a man, not a boy. This is good." Santino had changed too. Miguel barely saw a flicker of what had once been his cousin. This agitated man with hollow, sunken eyes seemed like a stranger; a serious, dark, unhappy stranger.

Leaning forward, Santino began, "I wanted you to come here to discuss business. It's time for you to take your place in my operation; to grow my business. I can make you a wealthy man. To begin, you will create new avenues to get my products to their destination. The American military can be very cooperative. This is where your work will begin."

"Santino, I'm glad that you trust me. But, it doesn't have to be this way. There are more than enough people who want to help you grow your business on every street corner."

"This is how it is, Miguel. It's simple—You are either with me, or you are against me. And, I won't have you against me."

"You are better than this, Cousin." The words tasted like vinegar in his mouth.

"The gringos need their drugs, Miguel. Someone will provide them with what they need—most likely someone more "wicked" than myself." Miguel had decided long ago that there was no one more despicable than his own cousin.

"I chose this life when it was the only way to survive. Now, I choose to thrive. This is the only way. My business creates jobs and income, something the Mexican government cannot do for our people. The government enslaves them in mines or leaves them to starve."

Miguel said, "You are rationalizing your behavior. You act as though you care about the people, yet you steal the kidneys of innocent babies. You torture…"

"Enough!!" Santino shouted. Miguel watched his cousin struggle to regain his composure. "You will judge me? You, who sits here with nothing that I have not given you! Where have you been for four years? Murdering enemies of *el Norte*? America is its own enemy. She will sell herself, give herself away, until she is nothing. I cannot save anyone. You did not save anyone. But, I have saved myself. And, I will save you when you join me."

"And if I don't?" Miguel asked.

Santino shrugged, "I will kill you. There is no other choice."

Miguel sipped at his beer while attempting to steady his trembling hand. He nervously looked around the room, stalling, though he didn't know what he was waiting for. The outcome of this conversation had been predetermined the day Papi had been given the farm.

At the bar, Santino's men were deep in conversation. They chatted, while Miguel wasted his last moments as a free man attempting to suppress a surging sense of panic. Miguel could see that one man was distracted. Each time Maria came into view, preparing the bar with fresh bottles and clean glasses, the man stood a little taller, separating himself by a half step from the other three. Marcos was the son of a very important family in the cartel. He was a young man, about to turn twenty-one but older than Maria who was only thirteen. He shouldn't be paying so much attention to Maria, Miguel thought.

"Your daughter. I want… perhaps you will allow me to take her back to Arizona with me for a while," Miguel said with forced optimism. "She will be safer with me than here. I'd like to have a chance to know the only family I have left. It's just me and Papi since I was thirteen. I haven't even seen *Abuela* since then."

Santino's eyes narrowed. "One minute you judge, the next… you want." Santino sat back in the chair again and folded his hands behind his head. "I will try not to feel the sting of your insult. Gabriella's needs are met in my home, and my daughter looks well. What makes you think she isn't safe?"

"I think, Santino," Miguel said through gritted teeth, "that you have kept Gabriella as a means of eventually manipulating me. And, your daughter is currently safe because she is still a virgin, and therefore, worth more to you. They are nothing but instruments for doing business to you. Much like I meant nothing to you personally. We are not family. I am an opportunity."

Santino waited before speaking again. He seemed to be considering something. "Those are bold statements to make, Miguel. Maybe you will be a better businessman that I have anticipated. You are with me then?" Santino asked grimly as though it were really a question.

"I am."

Santino's demeanor relaxed, but he maintained the air and expression of a victor—cold and superior. He slowly drew his cell phone from his pocket and dialed while carefully examining Miguel's face. "Let him go," he said and hung up the phone.

Miguel's eyebrows pushed involuntarily together as he pondered the meaning of Santino's statement. "Let him go," echoed in his mind until, like a punch in the gut, he knew that Papi was being released from jail. His eyes rolled behind his closed lids while he tried to absorb the relief of knowing that Papi would go home. But his chest tightened and stomach turned as he realized that Santino had had his father arrested. "You are a monster."

Santino watched Miguel and finally said, "I am a businessman. It's that simple."

"You are the devil."

"That is no attitude to begin a business relationship with, Miguel. I'll tell you what. To show you that I am fair, I will give you what you've asked for. Take Maria back to the farm. Get to know her and then you will begin working for me. Salute."

4

Maria

It was easy for Maria to get used to Miguel's silky brown hair and handsome face on the flight to Arizona, but she wasn't comfortable with him—not at all. Having seen men at their worst, she knew enough to be nervous.

"Is this your first flight, Maria?" She affirmed that it was with a slight nod of her head and returned her attention to her book.

"What are you reading?"

"The Alchemist."

"It's breaking apart. You're about to lose some pages."

"It's an old book. I've read it many times."

"What kinds of things would you like to do when we get to America?"

Maria thought for a moment. "I have never seen the ocean. I'd like to see a movie, you know, in a theater. I'd like to meet some friends my age. I would try some new things. Someday, I want to go to college."

Instantly, Miguel felt sad. It was a basic list really. He wondered if any of it would be possible for her. It was more likely that Santino would arrange for Maria to be married, and she would have no choice in the matter. Gabriella used to have a list of dreams as well, one of which had been going to college. He wondered if Gabriella was well. Being a prisoner is bad enough, but having Maria's life prescribed by Santino must be awful for her too.

Miguel decided not to ask too many questions. He needed time to earn Maria's trust, but he had liked her right away. Instead, he filled the time with his own stories. He talked about how he and Gabriella had been best friends when they were her age. "Your mother was sweet and funny. She was always teasing me. She had dreams too, like yours. She wanted to go to college."

"Mama says the same things about you, but she said that you always teased her."

A smile grew across Miguel's face as he gently repeated, "She… teased me." Maria smiled too and turned her attention to the puffy white clouds out the window.

A banged up, bruised Papi met them at the airport. Miguel face tensed when he saw the damage, and he hugged Papi gingerly. Miguel introduced Maria, and the two grinned at each other. Maria explained that she knew Papi already. "Your father has been my father's guest at Absinthe. Hello, Mr. Garces." She said shyly. He pulled her in for a hug. Miguel guessed by the expression of surprise on her face that this was their first hug.

"Call me Sal or Papi. Okay, Maria?"

"Sure."

***

Miguel didn't know what to do with Maria once he finally had her settled into her room at the farm. He had never cared for a child before. She wandered the house like a ghost, examining Papi's magazines and testing all the furniture.

"Can I get you something to drink?" Miguel asked tentatively.

"No, thanks."

"Want to play *fútbol*? I can show you how to make a ball like when I was a kid."

"I don't know how to play. Do you need me to do anything?"

"No, Maria. Think of our time together as vacation. No work for you."

"Can I go swing in the hammock over there? And, read my book?"

"Sure you can. But, that's not the same book. What are you reading now?"

"Ann Frank. Have you read it?"

"Uhhh. No. It wasn't required reading when I went to school. Why would you be reading about her?"

"It was just one of the books we collected; me and the other girls I live with. We have a little library of books." Maria shifted back and forth on her feet, inching closer to the door. Miguel thought she seemed eager to end the conversation. "Can I go now?"

"Right. Sure. Go ahead. I'll see you later."

Papi was still laughing when Miguel discovered him in the kitchen. "What? What's so funny?"

"Feeling a little awkward with a kid around, eh?"

Miguel laughed too. "Yes. A lot awkward. She's uncomfortable, Papi." Miguel shook his head. "It's difficult for her to look me in the eye. I thought it would be beneficial for Maria to come here, but I am beginning to doubt myself. I have no idea what this girl has experienced in her short life in México. Does she even know what required school reading is?"

"Be patient. Maria has only just arrived. Be patient and God will be your guide. It will be okay. Why not take her for a horseback ride around the farm?"

"That's a good idea. I wonder if she can ride."

***

Maria was eager to ride. She looked at Miguel with a puzzled expression as he hastily gathering blankets and saddles while she quietly brushed Buttercup.

"Something on your mind, Maria?"

"No, I just don't use a saddle," Maria bashfully contributed.

"You ride bareback?" Miguel didn't know anyone who rode that way. He could tell by her timid response that Maria didn't understand that she possessed a unique talent that few others could boast of. He had decided not to take anything for granted. Maria's way of life was completely different even though she and Miguel called the same place home for their first thirteen years.

"*Sí*. Mama taught me."

Miguel wondered what else Gabriella had taught Maria. He couldn't remember if Gabriella rode bareback when they were friends. "I'm glad we are going for a ride. I want to hear more about the things your mother has taught you." Maria smiled shyly and then slid out of sight behind Buttercup.

Ears pinned and eyes wide, Buttercup was as surprised about this no-saddle thing as Miguel had been. But, Maria's soft hands and strong legs brought them to an agreement after a couple passes in the ring.

"I'm not sure I am happy about this. Buttercup may never let me ride her with a saddle again."

Once under way, Maria became chatty, asking questions about the trail and the farm. She looked especially pretty sitting atop her golden, doe-eyed mount. With Miguel's prodding, she shared stories about her life; her lonely, short little life. Miguel couldn't help but draw contrast between the harshness of her reality compared to his own at thirteen.

Miguel remembered school days, laughter and *fútbol* games in the local field. He recalled birthday parties with piñatas, homework, chores, and Mass on Sunday. He looked forward to

Christmas more than any other holiday, but the Grand festivals were the most fun.

Everyone would fill the streets with carefree laughter and drunken revelry. Dancers in brightly colored costumes would twirl and sway through the streets in a wonderful, long parade. Fathers would ask mothers to dance with a bow and a kiss on the hand, and mothers softly bent their knees into a curtsy. They floated easily together and smiled all the while. Boys chased girls, who pretended a kiss would offend them, until the kiss was delivered and met both with a giggle and a slap in return.

Dogs were always stealing food from the tables and being chased away. Together, the whole community proudly and tearfully sang the national anthem. The fireworks would go off at midnight, but the darkness would blend with daybreak before the party was done.

All of his memories included Gabriella. Miguel recalled how she would throw her head back in euphoric laughter and tease him relentlessly. He would flex his arm presenting newly sculpted muscles, bragging about hair filling in everywhere it should. And, she often left one extra button unfastened, revealing her newly blossoming cleavage. He loved becoming a man and delighted in doing so with Gabriella. Thirteen had been a magical time for Miguel.

Maria had no stories of school or romance, but she did know how to restart the heart of a meth addict. She knew how to cut coke and draw lines. She could make a heavy-handed, alcohol-laden refreshment better than anyone and kept bar like her life depended on it.

She didn't know her father, Santino, other than by sight, and she feared him. He had given orders that no man touch Maria, but only because, as custom demands, she would bring a better price as a virgin "when the time comes." She feared "that time" was coming. Once, when she was ten years old, she spoke back to a customer, and her father had her caged for several nights with other hostages. It was too painful for her to talk about.

Miguel stopped his horse abruptly. An image of this sweet girl locked in a cage filled his head. Hate pushed up from somewhere inside him and he wanted to scream. He could barely hold back his rage toward Santino. He couldn't speak as the faded old image of his beautiful friend, his lovely Gabriella, being forced to the ground and raped crystallized in his mind.

Maria noticed the tension as Miguel squirmed in his saddle and asked if he was all right.

"I'm sorry, Maria. I'm sorry. I just needed a minute. That story was a shock. It's not easy to hear some things. A child's life should be filled with love and friendship and discovery. Every child deserves that. I'm okay now. Can you tell me more? I like the sound of your voice."

She explained that the older girls had taught her how to stay out of trouble and to pay attention to everything. She had learned how to make the dancers look sexy, with their lips painted red and hairpieces worn in shiny, long locks. She could sew or mend a costume in no time at all. She had no stories of playtime.

Gabriella had worked to keep Maria caught up with her studies. They rode horses in the ring together sometimes. They practiced speaking English, and Maria was learning to play the piano. One of the guards, Frankie, allowed mother and daughter to sleep together at the big house when Santino was away, but for the most part, she would spend her time with the other girls from the club.

Maria bragged that her mother had graduated high school on-line and studied other things, too. Gabriella played chess with Frankie, one of the more pleasant guards, and let him win occasionally so he wouldn't feel too bad. Miguel could see Maria glow with pride as she talked about her mother.

Several pleasant hours passed on horseback with Maria at her ease, and Miguel was grateful for this gift. Gradually, as they leisurely toured the farm, he learned about Maria and Gabriella, the business, the estate and the club. All of it might be helpful in the future. Maria was able to look Miguel in the eye from that afternoon on.

***

Miguel planned time each day to spend with Maria. Sometimes they prepared meals together; neither were very skilled at it, although they pretended that they were. Sometimes they practiced painting on canvas or scraps of wood. Miguel reminded Maria, "There is beauty in everything. Don't be too critical." Maria would smile as though something was funny as she admired his work, tilting her head like a puzzled puppy. They would both end up laughing. Miguel was better at teaching Maria how to start a garden, something in which she had little interest. She coaxed him play chess with her. She said he would be motivated to learn faster if she didn't let him win, and she didn't.

One afternoon Maria strode past Miguel, book in hand. He loved how comfortable she was becoming. She didn't ask permission anymore. She had taken on the air of a family member who knew what to do and did it.

He stood up and watched her plant herself onto the bench swing. He loved the way she wiggled her bottom, scooting herself against the back rest. She would fold her feet under her knees and with an expression of satisfaction, open her book. From a distance, it appeared to be the same tired, old book she was reading on the plane. He began to wonder if it was and why she would be reading it again.

Miguel stepped out into the sunshine and slowly walked to the bench. Maria noticed him approaching and closed the book. Together, they rocked. Maria wore a playful grin, repeatedly glancing at Miguel as though waiting for him to speak. She enjoyed his company immensely and didn't try to hide the fact.

"Where do you get your books?"

"Jazmin, mostly." Miguel's puzzled expression urged her to continue. "She manages things. She is like a mother figure to the girls. She controls the amount of drugs they get which keeps them from overdosing and committing suicide. When we are sick,

Jazmin gets us medicine. The rumor is that she used to work like the rest of the girls when she was young, but now that she is old, no one wants her, so she manages the club.

According to Jazmin, we girls need to learn everything we can. She says that good luck is when preparation meets opportunity. She brings books and speaks English to us when no one can hear her. She found us a laptop and hooked it up to the Internet, but she only lets us watch documentaries and school stuff. We can't use Facebook and the other fun sites. If anyone ever escaped because Jazmin helped them get online, she would be killed."

"What are you reading today? Is that the same book from the plane?"

"It is. It's called *The Alchemist*. It's about a shepherd boy who pursues his personal legend."

"A personal legend?" Maria laughed at the sincerity in Miguel's voice as she turned the pages to find one that she had bent at the corner. She read: "…whoever you are, or whatever it is that you do, when you really want something, it's because that desire originated in the soul of the universe. It's your mission on earth."

"And that means?" Suddenly Miguel felt like the teenager.

"We must endure the hardness of life whether we cower in fear or blaze our own trail. The trick is learning to live in the present while following our dreams and discovering our personal legend." Maria was excited to share this story and continued without missing a beat. "It means you have to test yourself. Contentment is sometimes the absence of courage. We accept our circumstances so that we don't have to try hard. When we try and fail, we feel as though the bad that follows is our own fault. That feels awful. But, when we let bad things happen and don't do anything about them, we blame someone else. Somehow it is less scary to live with the bad than it is to try to fix things, possibly failing. We are so afraid of losing, we never fulfill our dreams.

Wait, here is another quote, "We are afraid of losing what we have, whether it's our life or our possessions or our property. But this fear evaporates when we understand that our life stories and the history of the world were written by the same hand.'" Maria, in possession of Miguel's astonished attention, went on.

"I want to go to college, so I learn English and study what I can. That's all I can do for now. I was afraid to come here with you, away from Mama, but this trip also felt like one of Santiago's quests. He's the main character of the book. I had to find courage, so I brought this book with me, and now I am glad I came."

Miguel stared at the ground while processing the theory Maria had introduced and then asked, "Does the book explain how you know what your personal legend is?"

Maria knew exactly what to look for and swiftly found another page. "Every search begins with beginner's luck," she read. "And every search ends with the victors being severely tested." In other words, you don't always know. I think it changes along the journey anyway. The key is to start. When something is nagging at you, don't ignore it. Follow it. Begin your journey. It's the universe that speaks to you.

Maria fanned the book and stopped at another dog eared page. She read, "'Before a dream is realized, the Soul of the World tests everything that was learned along the way. It does this not because it is evil, but so that we can, in addition to realizing our dreams, master the lessons we've learned as we've moved toward that dream. That's the point at which, as we say in the language of the desert, one dies of thirst just when the palm trees have appeared on the horizon." Do you see? We are better off when the blame falls onto ourselves. This way, we learn. Next time, we will do better. Many of the bad things that happened to you aren't your fault, Miguel." Looking up to catch Miguel's eye, Maria spoke to him with the sweetest sincerity. "If you haven't already, you should begin your journey. The bad things may be your fault sometimes, but so will the good things. Every person's life is part of the entire world story. Everything is balanced together." She watched Miguel thoughtfully attempting to digest the ideas that she had explained.

"In the book, Santiago travels through Spain, into Africa, and to the pyramids of the Sahara desert, but he figures out that what he was searching for is a tree back at home where he originally started. He just couldn't have known that without having taken the journey. It does seems weird to me that his trip took him all over the place, just so he could end up laying around back under his favorite tree. But, he changed and learned all kinds of things. He is better for having taken the journey."

Flabbergasted and overwhelmed Miguel had run out of questions and sat quietly considering all that Maria had shared. He was inspired by her intelligence and maturity.

Maria filled what was, for her, an awkward silence, "All the girls love to read; mostly the classics from México and America, but anything really. Sometimes we act out scenes from the books which is fun. I don't have to… I don't have to work like the other girls do, so I have the most time to read. I read out loud to the girls, especially when they are sad or coming down from a real serious party night. They don't like to be alone then; they shake real bad and cry. The stories make them think of other exotic people and places. They say it gives them freedom."

The images of Maria caring for the shaking girls upset Miguel. His heart was aching and filled with love for this strong, introspective little lady. Finally he said, "I have an idea. Let's go into town tomorrow and buy some books to take home with you. I'll buy my own copy of *The Alchemist* and you pick out whatever you want."

"That would be great." Maria smiled. "I already know what I want."

"Are you going to tell me?"

"*I Am Malala.* Do you know who she is, Miguel?"

"Geez Maria. I know of her. Don't you ever read stories about puppies or boys?"

Maria let go a hardy laugh as she scooted over to him. He wrapped his arm around her shoulder, kissing her forehead as he did. Maria opened her book once again.

***

Miguel decided against driving to the little town for Maria's first shopping trip, and instead they headed to one of the nearest big cities, an hour away. Maria had never seen an American mall before, and he wanted her to be impressed.

Maria had not been allowed to shop just for fun, and she certainly had never seen the likes of an ice-cream shop with fifty flavors. They made themselves ill, testing as many flavors as they could.

There was so much to see and hear with advertisements in every direction, soft music filling the silence. This mall was new, clean, and the air was cooled by air conditioning. Because Maria appeared tentative, Miguel asked if she was all right. Having seen some of the old factories back home in México which were quite large yet windowless and uninviting, Maria confessed that she had never experienced anything like this mall.

Busy taking it all in, Maria had become very quiet. "I've never seen you speechless before, Maria." Miguel teased. "Well, not since you first arrived. You okay?"

Maria admitted reluctantly that she felt a bit uncomfortable, like she didn't belong there. She wondered why none of the shoppers were greeting each other or speaking at all. Everyone was awkwardly carrying bundles and bags, rushing silently by as they came and went.

"This place is nothing like the marketplace back home. The marketplace is always crowded with conversation and laughter, with people bargaining for the best price. It's warm and familiar. I feel like a ghost in this mall. I don't like it." Maria stood shaking her head.

Miguel felt disappointed, having hoped that Maria would be excited. He asked if she wanted to shop in any of the clothing stores, to which she responded with a surprising lack of enthusiasm. But, once they had passed all of the scented candles, nauseating perfume shops and handlers of free lotion samples, they arrived at the book store and Miguel received the reaction he had anticipated. Maria became animated as she moved briskly around the tables. He had trouble following her stride. She covered her face with her hands as excitement overtook her.

He was pleased. Never had Maria seen so many books. "Where do I begin?" she exclaimed.

"Can I help you find something? What are you looking for?" A twenty-something sales clerk with rings on every finger and a bejeweled lip, tongue and nostril had overheard Maria.

"Yes, you can help. Maria's looking for a few new books." The clerk acknowledged Miguel with a nod of her head. "I am going to grab a quick cup of coffee. Have fun, girls." Maria's eyes followed Miguel as he strode toward the cafe which was nestled into the front corner of the store. They had passed it on their way in, though she had not noticed it.

Miguel intermittently peeked at Maria and the salesgirl, as he prepared his coffee and found a table to revel in the pleasure of watching Maria's delight. At first, she was hesitant to engage the clerk, but shortly Maria became absorbed by her. He watched them build a stack in Maria's arms until she could no longer carry them, and they transferred the mound to the floor instead. The clerk frequently disappearing behind the rows, reemerging with new selections for Maria, who had plopped herself down cross-legged on the floor. As she finished each examination, she placed the books into piles. The selections in queue to be read lay heavily across her lap, making her appear to be a torso with no legs.

When Miguel returned, she explained that she had divided the books into three groups, "yes," "no" and "maybe" piles. Miguel, while helping to put the "no" and "maybe" piles away, asked, "Do you think you can narrow it down to five selections? More than that and your luggage might be too heavy for the plane. If you can't decide, maybe we can come back another day." Maria smiled, but Miguel sensed that she might be considering if he would be able to keep that promise. He wondered the same thing as well.

"I can see that, *I Am Malala* will be coming home with us. What else have you chosen?"

"Well, it was hard to decide. At first I was searching for stories about people my age. Reading about kids makes me feel like I have friends which is nice. Then I thought I should travel the world with my new books and tried to find something from each continent, but that was too hard. Jazmin says I should learn about other cultures in case I ever get away from Santino, so that was on my mind. I ended up with, *To Kill a Mockingbird*, *The Secret Garden*, *1984*, *The Art of War* and of course, *I Am Malala*." She pointed to each title as the cashier rang up the total.

"I was thinking that next time you come, we might consider a visit to the library."

"Sure. Thanks. But, I know I will reread these." she protectively tucked the bag of books a little closer.

***

"What's going on there?" Maria asked on the ride home.

"It looks like a protest to me. I read that the President is speaking today."

"Do you know what he's talking about?"

"I think mostly, he's making promises he won't keep," Miguel laughed. "That's why some of the people are gathering. He's going to talk about people like you and me. People who come here to the states because their own homes have been devastated. He says he wants to give us money, but he is really just trying to buy votes. We'll never see any money. It's not that different from Mexican politics really. Business influences the voting here, cartels influence the voting there."

"I think that is a good idea, giving people who need it money to live better."

"Maybe so," said Miguel, "but where's the money going to come from? What if everyone who is hurting in México wants to come here? What will become of our beautiful México? And, what will become of this country? What about the people in the Middle East and Malala? Should all of Syria come too? They are all suffering."

"I don't know." Maria admitted. "I never thought about it that way. That would be millions of people and I don't even know how much money. I hope you won't laugh at me, but someday I would like to be a president."

"You certainly dream big, Maria."

"I would just tell people not to use drugs, and then, they can get and keep jobs. Santino and his henchmen will fade away and disappear. No one will be scared anymore."

"Well, you have to be born here to be president, why not become president of México?"

Miguel could tell that she was lost in thought while considering that possibility. Maria had finally run out of questions and sat quietly next to him. Lids heavy, she rested her head on his shoulder and drifted off to sleep, her arms still hugging the bag of new books.

5

The Plan

"Papi, come on. Let's walk." Miguel's feet scuffed the dirt, startling a previously motionless lizard. He watched it waddle away. Miguel's hands pushed their way deep into his pockets like two nervous rabbits hiding in their den.

"Are you digging around in those pockets to find your courage or your *cajones*?" Papi asked with a laugh. Miguel laughed too and liberated his hands. Papi had always been direct, and Miguel found it to be a comfort.

Miguel scanned the horizon as though the incentive he needed to begin speaking might be found there. The mesas and buttes reminded him of death, not the optimism for which he was searching. He realized that it actually might have been the lush mountain range of México that he had hoped to see. He would have to follow Papi's example and be direct.

"Papi. I don't know what to do."

"What's troubling you, Son?"

"My responsibility will be to distribute drugs through the military for Santino. He said wants me to do another tour if I have to, just to make sure things go smoothly."

"You're not going to have to do that though, right?"

"I can't do it, Papi. I can't do another tour. He says he will get me "strategically placed," so it will be an easy time, but I can't. I hated it. There were times when I was over there, I would be positioned to defend a building, and I would just hope for a bullet to strike me. I couldn't run out in to the street to make it happen because I would have endangered my troop, but I wanted to. I would close my eyes and pray for a bullet to rip my head off."

"Why are you talking like that? Why would you want to die?" Miguel could see that his words had shroud Papi's face in sadness.

"Papi, it hurts. Everyday. Every time I think of them. I wonder how long Mama and Juan lay in that desert before they died." Miguel felt like his heart might burst just saying this aloud. "We never buried them, Papi. I regret leaving them. We should have died with them. It would have been more courageous than what we did."

"Don't speak of it! It's done." Tears poured from Papi's eyes as he shouted.

"I have to. You don't want to talk about it, but I have to." Miguel could see that his words were torturing Papi. Miguel began to understand the depth of the guilt that Papi suffered with. It was clearly a heavy burden to him.

"I was there, Miguel. It was the hardest thing I have ever done. God forgive me. I don't speak of bullets. I have regret, but live with what I did. One day at a time, I live with it."

Miguel continued, "I didn't know what happened to Gabriella. My heart ached to know if she lived or died. And, now that I know she's alive, everything has changed for me. Now that I have met Maria, I can't send her back. How could I send that beautiful child back to that savage? I want to save her as much as you wanted to spare me in the desert. I want her to have some happiness. I don't want to live with more regret.

And, I want no part of Santino's business. His business devastated my family, my home and even my pride in being Mexican. It's taking the United States down, too. It's a slow process, but I see it everywhere. Before long, there will be no place for anyone to run."

"I have prayed it wouldn't come to this," Papi said. "But, I don't think you have another choice, my son. You have to do Santino's work, or he will kill you."

"I have to find another option. I have to make another choice. I won't be part of it. Do you think we can fight back? Do you think we could put Santino out of business?"

"No. I don't. You're talking like a crazy man, and I want you to stop. If you go to war with Santino, you're a dead man. You're all I have left, Miguel. I can't lose you. Please, don't talk like this, Son. Santino will make you a wealthy man. You will have no worries after I am gone. When I know you have wealth and can take care of yourself, I can die in peace."

Miguel's eyes widened with consternation, "I won't have any worries? Are you serious? Santino is not going to protect me; he's going to use me. I will be killed eventually anyway. He will try to lure me in; to make me a killer. And, when I refuse to kill for him, I'll be dead. It's a trap."

Papi knew what his son said was true. Miguel would survive for a while. But, he would never truly be alive again, not in his soul. He would live in shame. The dignity of a free man would never be his. He would never feel safe.

"Don't you realize that Gabriella and Maria would be killed for spite. He'd kill me too, Miguel. You'd need an army, and guns and a friggin' miracle from God himself. You're going need a bullet proof plan, because you certainly are not."

Miguel listened carefully to his father's words. He could see desperation in his father's eyes. But, he had seen despair in Maria's eyes as well. "We confiscated a great deal of weapons overseas," Miguel said. "They are stored in warehouses all around over there. We all know that sometimes the weapons are rerouted back to the enemy in trade. Usually they are traded for drugs. Maybe I could arrange it. Maybe, I could trade drugs for weapons and put them in the hands of the people of our village. Do your remember Pedro from back home? I served overseas with him for a while. He's a heavy user, and he's made those kinds of deals. He'd be willing to do something for me."

"Do you know how many weapons you would need? And, Santino's going to want his money, Miguel. He's going to want his money."

"I know. I know. I need to think. There has to be a way. If I do what he wants, I'm going to ruin the rest of my life, and I won't to able help Gabriella and Maria. If I don't, I will have no life to ruin. There has to be another option. I have to think of something. It's time, Papi. The time for change has come."

Turning back toward home the two men walked along the road, watching daylight change to brilliant shades of red and orange at the horizon. The light refused to yield to darkness, celebrating the day that had passed with an impressive reminder of the gifts that light and life bring. The colorful sky filled their hearts with both gratitude and sorrow as day gave way to night.

Papi spoke carefully, as though choosing his words one by one. "*Mi hijo*, my son. You are courageous. I am proud of the man you have chosen to be." Miguel could see that his father's words, heavy with pride, were choking him, but it was the guilt that Papi had been carrying for years that strangled him. "You're brave and strong, kind and good." Papi placed his hands on Miguel's shoulders. "You are everything your mother had hoped you would be. Please forgive me. Please. I wish I had been stronger. I wish I could have saved them both. I'm sorry I couldn't protect you. I am sorry it has come to this." Miguel's heart ached for his father. He pulled Papi close and embraced him.

"I forgive you, Papi. I am proud of you. You did what you had to do." He kissed his father's tearful cheeks. Miguel was overwhelmed. Papi had been suffering in silence, in despair, all this time. Miguel had been absorbed in his own pain. His father's burden, once spoken, felt dense and crushing. Too heavy to be carried by one man for so long, Miguel wished he had not been so blind, so selfish.

Regaining his composure slowly, Papi seemed worn out, yet relieved. Miguel kept an arm around his father's shoulder, and Papi placed his around Miguel's back. Miguel could remember walking like this when he was a boy, in México. They would finish their chores and walk back home, spent and dirty, arm in arm. It was a comfort, one of life's simple, sweet pleasures.

"Your name suits you well." Papi began. "I am thinking of Padre Miguel Hidalgo y Costilla and his cry for revolution from that little town of Dolores so long ago. His war lasted eleven long years, but he did achieve the independence our ancestors so desperately craved. I couldn't be more proud of you for endeavoring to take a stand. I think it's time to tell you the story about how we evaded death on that terrible journey across the desert sands to end up here."

"You said a man with a truck drove across the sand to rescue us."

"That's true in the end. He was an angel from heaven, and I remain forever grateful to him. But, I believe that it was by God's design that we lived through that quest for freedom from the cartel." He paused a long while before speaking again. It was punishing for Papi to think back through those memories, and harder still to make his mouth say the words.

"It was almost dawn. I was sure that I had taken my last step. Shivering with cold, a cold that consumed me, I rolled onto my back to die. With my face to heaven, I prayed and prayed. I made peace with God and thanked him for all the blessings of my life, for the time he had given me. As I waited for the relief that death would bring, a drop of water landed on my forehead. And then, another. The rain didn't last long, but I stretched out the piece of parchment, and with it, I filled our bottle with enough water to recover some strength and walk on with you by my side.

I don't know how much time passed, but that miracle inspired my thought and guided my steps the rest of the way. I wondered why we were being spared. I wondered what purpose God had for us. I had promised him that I would be his dedicated servant for the rest of my life. But, I haven't fulfilled my promise. Perhaps this is my time to make good on it."

Miguel agreed that as difficult as God's intentions were to comprehend, he might have chosen them on that day to do some good, something no one else could do. Father and son walked on, lost in thought but found in God's grace. They felt peace.

***

That night, after Maria was tucked in bed for the night, Miguel and Papi conspired endlessly until the humble beginnings of a complex scheme to end Santino's rein of terror was finally born. They both knew that the United States consume more than seventy percent of all illegal drugs produced and that the number would only increase. Americans love their drugs and had the money to spend. As long as there was a demand, there would be a supply. That was not something that a small band of rebels could affect. But, Miguel and Papi hoped was that their war could end the terror the cartels used to control people.

"Our message will be that drug cartels can claim their industry, but they have to do it without terrorizing Esperanza. Both can exist without damage to the other. We're not trying to put the cartels out of business. We only want to be safe in our neighborhoods once again," Miguel said.

"The drug world involves more people than we can count," Papi offered. "Most politicians, police, and judges are under the cartels' influence, even when they resist. If we damage Santino's cartel enough, we will provide an opportunity for the government to take back some control. People live in fear of being killed, even while doing the work of devils. There's no mercy. There's only power through the use of terror. If people are smart, they will take advantage of the opportunity to break free when we hand it to them."

"The drug business generates more wealth than the major corporations of the US. That money is going to be our biggest enemy." Miguel countered.

"Once our people are armed, the kidnapping has to stop," Papi said. "I am sure many people will still accept bribes, but when the gangs are unable to raid villages because the villagers are armed, there will be a shift in the balance of power."

"People who joined the drug world out of desperation or were forced into the business will have a way out."

The biggest problem for Miguel and Papi to overcome was that no person was of any real value in the cartels. No matter who Miguel's resistance struck, a willing replacement would pop up like a weed by the next day. Those in power worked to maintain their power, but everyone was expendable. Miguel and Papi couldn't and didn't want to kill thousands of people. They would have to concentrate on making an impressive effort in a single area, the town of Esperanza.

"The priority is getting the captive children out and back to their parents, if we can find them. If they are still alive." Papi said, "I'll bet some still have family alive somewhere. The church will be of no help with "The Executioner" there. I'd like to be the one to take him out. I would really like that."

"If some of the croppers from here at the farm go back and fight, and if I can arm the merchants and villagers, maybe we have a chance," Miguel said. "I think the key will be the element of surprise. That's how the cartel does it. If we knew when they were going to invade our towns, the losses wouldn't be so extensive. The cartel won't be expecting anyone to rebel."

"I know some of our farm workers would go back to México and fight to have our lives back, but let's not get carried away.

How are you going to get croppers back over the border with weapons?" Papi asked.

Miguel considered this question for a long while. "We'll load them into trucks and say that we suspect the Fever is among them. We'll say we are sending them all back before the Centers for Disease Control and Prevention, CDC, can get involved. No one will check a truck with Fever in it. We'll just have to connect with the right border patrol guard and provide enough incentive."

"Okay. That might work," Papi said. "So, you will make the arrangements with Pedro to get weapons into México. Do you remember Sharkie, the local mechanic? He will be able to help us hide and distribute them. Santino will be satisfied that you're working when you tell him about the drug shipment, but when he doesn't receive his money that will be the biggest problem. Timing this is going to be a nightmare, and I am afraid that all be in vain. Do you think we should burn some of the fields while we are at it? Cutting into their profits would get their attention."

Miguel asked, "Can you fill your plane with that chemical and spray 'em? Can you imagine spraying all of the fields with that crap? Nothing would ever grow there again," he snorted and began to chortle, "except soybeans, maybe." He laughed a long, hardy laugh. Tears pushed out of his eyes. "Soybeans and corn."

His joy was contagious and Papi joined in, too, which made Miguel laugh harder. Even if this momentary release was caused by nervousness, Miguel knew that they were doing the right thing. No matter the result, it would be worth the effort. "Maybe we can be proud Mexicans again. It won't be the same, but we will have more honor than the way we live now." Miguel concluded optimistically.

***

When it was time for Maria to return to México, Miguel gave her two cell phones and two chargers to hide in her luggage, along with her new books. She promised to get one of the phones to her mother.

Miguel told her, "The password is 'love,' Maria. There is a message on this phone for your mother. She must see it and contact me when it's safe. It is important to make sure the phones never ring. Keep the sound off, and check for messages whenever you can."

Maria understood and nodded. "I will."

"Sending you back to México is breaking my heart. I am going to miss you more than I ever could have imagined possible. You're beautiful, I love you."

Maria tried to be brave, but she cried. Leaving Miguel was breaking her heart, too. When she hugged him goodbye, she whispered, "I love you too, Papa." He felt her wet face land on his cheek with a kiss.

***

The club seemed darker and lonelier to Maria when she returned. Missing the warmth and sweetness of being with Miguel and Papi, she had a hard time focusing on her work.

Marcos made his presence known. He watched Maria like a father might watch a baby who had just learned to use her feet. While his usual companions busied themselves playing pool and hitting on women, he began a new routine of ordering his drinks at the bar. Maria had to serve him, but she avoided eye contact as much as possible. Marcos, and the attention he paid to her, was not totally unwelcome. Maria would have liked to have had his friendship. But, the knowledge that Santino was planning to give her to someone in marriage, without her consent, required that Maria keep her distance. She couldn't appear interested and she absolutely couldn't encourage him.

Living in a dark, tenement style apartment building provided by Santino, Maria and the other girls were always watched, but none of them were considered an escape risks. Most had been moved far away from their family homes when they were stolen; many were from different countries. Some had been taken at such a young age that they weren't sure of exactly where they were from. Esperanza and the apartment building was home, and the girls were family. Drug addicted, with little or no education, they really had no prospects for opportunity. They worked as prostitutes and strippers at parties and at the club, in exchange for food, shelter and drugs. Their tip money bought them clothes.

Maria didn't work by taking her clothes off. With her mother and Santino nearby, there was no place for her to run. She was able to go into town to shop for what she needed but she was always with the other girls who were accompanied by and a pair of Santino's men.

She was back in Esperanza, the place she had always considered home, but for the first time Maria's true home felt far away. This was the first time she longed to be with someone other than Gabriella.

6

Pulling it Together

Miguel's chest tightened when the phone rang, and he answered it on the first ring. He held it to his ear and listened hoping to hear Gabriella speak. He hoped she would have some sweetness left to her voice, but there was no sound and then the line went dead. A second time, the line went dead before he could utter a noise.

Miguel knew that Gabriella must have been as nervous to call him as he was to speak to her. The last time they saw each other was thirteen years ago when he had been in and out of unconscious, and she had been thrown into the street. Remembering all of it forced raw emotion to the surface.

Finally, upon answering, he said, "Hi Gabby." And she didn't hang up. He thought he could hear the quiet breath of someone crying. He waited. "It's okay, Gabs, I'm here. Talk to me." Heart racing, he listened to her sob softly.

"It's really good to hear your voice," she said.

"Your's too… it's still the same."

"Well, what did you think I would sound like?"

"I don't know," Miguel waited, anxious to hear her say something, anything that might make her seem real and near.

"So, I guess you're not taking me to the semi-formal…?"

Miguel had almost forgotten about the dance. It seemed a lifetime ago, but he easily recalled feeling proud and excited to be taking Gabriella. "No. I guess not." He said. "I hope to make it up to you one day." He waited for his old friend to quiet her tears and respond.

Gabriella had to be careful not to make too much sound as she would not be able to explain having a phone or to whom she was talking if discovered. They talked about Maria and how much Miguel had enjoyed her. She explained the details of her own life that might not break his heart.

"Listen" Miguel began. "I have agreed to work for Santino, but only because I don't really have a choice in the matter. Papi and I owe him a debt. Once that happens, there will be no way out. I have been thinking. I want to get you and Maria out of there. I know it sounds crazy, and I realize that I may get us all killed, but I want to shut him down. I want to be able to come home to México. Do you want that too?"

There was a long pause before Gabriella responded, "Yes. I want to be free again. I do. I just don't think you know what you are getting into. It's impossible."

"I don't think it is. We think an initial strike could get you out, including the girls being held captive. We want to free them."

"Whose "we"?"

"Me and Papi. My father, Salvador, is working with me. If we surprise the cartel, I think we can do it. It won't solve everything, but anything would be better than this. I can secure weapons enough for a strike, and a group of croppers who work here at the farm will be able to recruit others. We just need to take back control of our village, and then others will rise up. I know it. Murder and rape is taking its toll. People can't live like this forever. So many good men have ended up working for the cartels.

I know they will turn their guns in the right direction to get their freedom, too."

"And, what if it doesn't work?"

"We get out of there. We head south into the chaos of México City. Then, we figure it out from there. But, at least we will be free. And, we'll be together. I'll find a place where we can dance."

"You've always been a dreamer," Gabriella said. "Let me think about it. I have to protect Maria. I need time to think. " Their phones had begun beeping, a warning that the batteries had lost their charge. "We'd better hang up now."

"Sure Gabs. Let's talk again when you can."

"I'll be looking forward to it."

***

Miguel easily found the crowded pub where Pedro had agreed to meet. He could have followed the raucous sounds that drinking men make. With the military base nearby, he felt back-at-home. The order and structure at the base brought peace to his troubled mind. He felt his stride becoming relaxed and realized that he had missed being part of it.

A *fútbol* match on TV was punctuated with jocularity, toasts and cheering. Miguel shouted his beer choice at the bartender, through a dense crowd standing three-deep, and located a table near the corner. He kept his eyes on the nearest TV screen, but his thoughts were of Pedro and the dusty streets of Esperanza where *fútbol* had been their favorite pass-time.

Pedro was a couple years older but they had been good friends. Neighborhood kids played together regardless of age; they worked things out without a parent or referee. The ball was made of whatever scraps they could be cobbled and taped together. Once in a while, someone would be given a real ball, and the neighborhood played with that until it was no longer recognizable.

Miguel remembered back to the first time he had run faster than Pedro, an upper classman, in a race. It had been a proud moment until a black eye became his trophy. Pedro had sucker punched him in a moment of machismo, but Miguel didn't care. He had been faster and would be respected for it. After that, the two become best friends.

After Miguel left Esperanza, he didn't know what had become of Pedro, until they found each other stationed together overseas. Pedro hadn't looked good back then, with the exception of his big toothy grin.

Pedro's crossing to America had been painful. He had been alone, and the coyotes who crossed him were dishonest men. His parents hadn't been able to afford to leave México with him. His crossing and his life in America had been different from Miguel's, but it was just as empty.

Pedro had found that getting high eased his pain, and coke had become his best friend. He said the world became a beautiful place when he was high on coke, and the world should always feel like that. He said he had a handle on it.

Pedro's face lit up at the sight of Miguel, and they fell into a long embrace. "It's great to see you." Men who have been in battle together have a unique and unbreakable bond. They learn to depend on each other. Something happens, an alliance, deep inside.

As the two men sipped their beers, they spoke about life, and they laughed. Neither brought up anything unpleasant, though both could easily read between the lines. They had learned to read each other, eyes revealing as much as their words. Pedro knew Miguel had been holding something back.

Miguel could barely hide his happiness as he explained that he had found Gabriella and her daughter. But, then he told Pedro about Santino and Miguel's obligation to the business. Pedro was aware of Santino and his activities, but used other suppliers for his contraband. Santino was the reason that he, too, had abandoned México. Pedro didn't want to do business with Santino, but he always kept an ear open for information about his beloved hometown.

Miguel explained that Santino expected him to use connections, like Pedro, to open new markets for Sanino's drugs. He hoped Pedro could help, and Pedro agreed that he would. "For you, Miguel, I will. But, you have to know how much I don't want to support that man. My pass for leave is only for today, but my tour is up in a couple weeks. I'll take care of it. All it will take is a few phone calls."

"I am interested in something else," Miguel continued. "I want to get paid in weapons rather than cash. You know? Confiscated weapons from storage. I know you've done it. Can you help me and do it again?"

"Trading for weapons is easier than cash," Pedro said. "Whatever you need. I can get it."

"I'll need everything to fight a ground war, except the tanks." The two men's eyes locked. Neither man spoke while Pedro tried to grasp the scope his friend was planning to do.

"Okay." Pedro slowly replied. "I'll take care of you. When do you want the delivery?"

"As soon as possible. The drugs will ship after the weapons arrive. *Amigo*, these people are not looking to make any new friends under normal circumstances, so when Santino's people figure out their payment was weapons shipped but not received, there will be hell to pay. Understand?"

Pedro said with a chuckle. "This is your first deal then, right?"

"Likely to be my last, too."

"Don't worry about me. I will make myself invisible and be gone completely in a couple of weeks. You will be surprised to see how easy it is. There's a seller, a buyer and a distributor. I just have to hire the distributer. We are not inventing the process; it's well established.

Deals used to be much harder before the cartels. Everyone in the chain would take a bite, and half the cargo would fail to arrive at the intended destination. But, then the cartels were born and people started getting killed for stealing." Pedro shook his head and continued, "Usually when I say that someone has sold their soul, I mean after death the devil owns them. But with these guys, the soul is sold and claimed in the here and now. These guys are no longer human, you know? Whatever it is that makes us human, it doesn't exist for them. They will fuck you up if you cross 'em. You don't even want to know. But, I'm in good graces all around. Everybody gets what they want. I've got the power of the US military on my side," Pedro laughed. "Our good 'ole boys have been through too much. You know, you've been there. Nothing bonds a unit like a coke delivery. Our boys need it and the officers know it, so they look the other way. I'll make it work. Of course, there will be hell to pay when Santino doesn't get his money, but at least you'll have what you need."

Miguel didn't want to know any more about Pedro's plans than he had to. Pedro wouldn't let him down. They let the matter drop, poured another round from the pitcher on the table and rejoined the revelry. Pedro found a couple of friends in the bar and they all rehashed tales that got taller with every pitcher of beer.

***

Papi was a familiar face on the cotton side of the farm. At times, he had worked in the fields, and he had become friends with many of the men who came back to the farm from season to season. He was even friendlier with others who stayed on all year. Work was easier with Papi around. The men respected him.

Papi selected a few of the individuals with whom he was closest and over a few beers at the bunk-house fireplace, began to fashion his plan. The men became attentive and excited, struggling to be discrete. The new foreman looked like he might be part basset hound with his sniffing around and watching from a distance.

The croppers had often spoke of rebellion amongst themselves, but it was only talk, as they knew that they could never get far without weapons or money. They were skeptical, fear had been burned into their souls, but they were willing to listen. Papi was not a laborer. He was plotting to save others, a risk that could cost him dearly. He had everything to lose and that was all the croppers needed to know.

The workers who came from southern México said that resistance groups had been springing up for a few years. "People have had enough. The government always disarmed the coups, but not before they made their point with the gangs. Have you noticed the price of limes has come down? One of the cartel leaders actually went into hiding after an uprising. The police and military started pressuring the gangs, and the farmers didn't have to pay taxes to the cartel, so it's working. Those farms could afford to pay us, and we didn't have to come north."

This was encouraging news to Papi. He had been hearing some of the same stories, but they were hard to believe or invest in.

"What can you do for us? If we risk our lives to help you in Esperanza, what will you do for our families in the South?" one of the workers asked.

"I wish I could make promises to you. The truth is, I really don't know. We will be armed, but I don't know what we will have for supplies yet. This will work best if we take control in one area and spread out from there. All of México will get the message if we do this well. Just as fear mushrooms, rebellion multiplies, too." Papi could see that the men wanted more. They wanted assurance. But, their faces broadcasted their anger at the cartels, and that was all the confirmation he needed. He felt sure they would fight.

One of the workers, who also called Esperanza "home" said, "I know more than I want to about the drug business and the abduction business. We all do. We just don't have a way to fight back. I can show you the location of one of the production tents, and I know where a cache of weapons is stored. And, the kids; I know where they are."

"All right." Papi said, "That's a good place to start. Any of you who would normally leave the farm tomorrow, come by the house after work instead. I will have food ready, and we can go over some maps."

They touched glasses and toasted, "Viva México."

***

"When Santino travels, the house gets casual." Gabriella whispered into the phone. "That could be an opportunity. He's leaving next week for a few days. How soon can you be ready?"

"I have my contact in place for the weapons to be shipped." Miguel said. "The croppers here will be sent back soon to begin spreading the word among those who can be trusted. How many men does he usually travel with?"

"It depends. Maybe three. A bunch of guys go over to the club when Santino leaves—mostly the heads of families and their bodyguards. They take the night off, so to speak. They'll be high and barely walking on their way out. There'll be twenty or so anyway. Absinthe doesn't have cameras outside or inside because too much business is conducted there."

Maria told me they always park in the same spot near the parking lot exit. If you have your people there when they go in, you'll know who is in which car. You can then disable the cars and wait. The bodyguards will be fairly sober, so you'll shoot them first. The rest won't be physically able to react quickly and if all goes well, you'll have the vehicles to use when moving the kids to safety. You'll have their keys, their cash, and their credit cards. That would really be helpful."

Miguel was impressed with Gabriella's ability to remain calm and clear. Talking to her gave him the insight he needed. She was smart to find a vulnerability in the system. She knew Santino, his routines and his people. She knew that they would never expect any form of retaliation.

Santino's bribes kept politicians and police out of his way. His gangs terrorized the citizens often to keep them fearful. Fearful enough to never attempt challenging the cartel. The people were starved and broken, so they could never even hope to organize. This time though, the cartel's over-confidence and Gabriella's insight left a crevice just large enough for Miguel's little resistance group to crawl into and begin eroding Santino's comfort and security.

It was hard for Miguel to listen to Gabriella speak so easily about killing people. She was a long way from the girl who only worried about making straight A's in school and deciding what to be when she grew up. Gabriella's sweet voice filled his mind with images of a playful thirteen year-old girl whose long brown curls bounced when she walked and lifted in the wind. A girl whose face never lacked a soothing smile with eyes that suggested she was bursting with secrets that he needed to know. And then she would suggest shooting the bodyguards and stealing cars and his mind would fill with blank space. He could see only the room he was standing in; her face would disappear leaving a stranger's voice behind.

Miguel wondered if he had ever talked about taking a life with a woman or with anyone outside the military other than Papi. He was sorry that this path was the direction he had to take. He was sorry for so many things that had happened, things he had no control of. Having control and planning a massacre was a nightmare effort for him as he hated violence. As the time for action approached, the thought of committing murder made him twist a little inside his own skin. Taking a life was a painful, almost unbearable experience. Even when there were no other option, extinguishing a life would rattle his soul.

Gabriella suggested pulling Sharkie, the local mechanic, into the plan. "Sharkie, down deep inside, is a good man. That fact is not always obvious, but it makes a good foundation upon which to build a relationship. One would be hard pressed to call him honest, but he is not without honor when doing business."

Miguel said, "Sharkie's already on the team. He had already agreed to receive the weapons and stash them."

Sharkie had a large protected area for working on cars and trucks. He would store the weapons for a price, because he would store anything for a price. Having been bullied by the gangs like everyone else, Sharkie didn't need much encouragement to invest in the coming adventure.

Gabriella added that Sharkie could advise on the best way to temporarily disable the SUV's. Whatever was done to disable the vehicles, would have to be able to undone just as quickly.

During Miguel's short conversation, Gabriella never mentioned "a backup plan," should things go awry. So far, no one had talked about the possibility of failure, but Miguel was certain that it was lurking in everyone's thoughts. The consequence of an uprising would be catastrophic. There was no way to measure the certain destruction that would result from fighting back, especially if their plan went wrong. Gabriella spoke with confidence, yet she had the most to lose by challenging Santino.

Gabriella had always wondered why she was not forced to work at the club as a sex slave like all the other kidnapped girls. The first day after her capture, she thought Santino was keeping her safe. He had pulled her out of the group of girls himself before the rest were put into cages and some were shipped away. But, he had raped her on the second day and beat her when she had tried to speak to him.

The days had passed slowly as a prisoner, but the nights lagged endlessly on. No one was there to ease the pain and humiliation of being raped or quell the fear of footsteps approaching in the hallway. She was a mere child, still fearful of shadows in the night. Her body ached much like if she had been burning with fever, but she wasn't sick. She was desperately alone, except for fear, her constant companion, and the horror of Santino's periodic intrusion.

She would pass her delicate limbs through the bars on her window letting the sunshine touch her skin. No replacement for the warmth of a mother's love or Miguel's playful grin, it was a comforting caress none-the-less, helping her to survive.

Then there was movement in her abdomen and her tears turned off as quickly as a faucet. She felt hope. God was providing her with a companion. She thought back to stories the older women told back at home about child birth and wondered if she would survive it. Alone. At least the life in her belly was hers to grow, and she already loved it.

One of the men, Frankie, who guarded Gabriella's room allowed her to keep her door open during the day when Santino was away on business. Frankie, a middle aged man with a receding hairline and a rounded belly, was married but childless. He would make funny faces at Gabriella as he patrolled passed her room. She giggled so wildly that he had to rush his finger to his lips to quiet her. As the years passed and Gabriella grew older, Frankie brought her a chess board. Their games often lasted two hours at first. They both learned to play with more speed over time. Gifts of children's books for Maria became common. Gabriella thanked God for Frankie.

Santino had lost interest in Gabriella when her belly swelled, and he left her alone. She enjoyed six long years with her beautiful baby, Maria, and with Frankie, who pretended to keep a professional distance but truly had fallen in love with both of them. The day that Jazmin, the manager of the Absinthe, came to take Maria at the tender age of six to begin working at the club, Gabriella died inside. She screamed and begged for Jazmin's mercy. Patiently at first, Jazmin waited for the news to settle in, but when Gabriella pulled at Jazmin's shirt, as quick as a cobra, she struck Gabriella's face. Gabriella charged at Jazmin, who had picked Maria up. Frankie had to do his job and hold Gabriella back. Once Jazmin had left with Maria, Frankie held Gabriella and stroked her hair. He promised that it would be okay.

Gabriella had barely recovered when heavy footsteps fell in the hallway outside. Her eyes became wide with fear. Frankie peeled her off of him and pushed Gabriella away; she landed awkwardly on the floor. Frankie made it out her door, passing Santino just before he entered and locked it. Frankie's stomach lurched. He ran down the hallway, away from whatever sounds might escape her bedroom, into the nearest bathroom where he threw up until the heaving and retching finally gave way to tears.

Frankie kept his distance after that day. Gabriella knew that he was hurting, possibly as much as she was, and didn't press him. He arranged for Maria to come back to the house on nights when Santino would be away or otherwise occupied. If Maria didn't work the next day, the girls could spend time together. Gabriella would speak English to Maria. She taught her to read, play chess, kept her up on her studies, and when Frankie had the time, they rode horses in the training ring. Frankie gave Gabriella a laptop to help fill her empty time with internet access to one site; a site to study for a high school equivalency test. It was a tremendous risk for him, but her gratitude made the gamble worthwhile.

Gabriella might have lost her mind if not for the bits of freedom Frankie offered. And now, Miguel's temptation of true freedom breathed new life into her. Miguel was not going to be stopped. She would have to ignore the fear that, through conditioning, came first.

***

Papi borrowed two canvas covered trucks and packed thirty men into each. Guns and ammunition had been sewn into blankets and clothes. They shoved more weapons into hollow parts of the truck, between the inside and outside panels of the bumpers and fenders. They loaded food, water, some cash, ambition and courage. The men possessed such courage. The possibility of restoring their dignity emboldened them. The fact that they had each other made the coming battle something they looked forward to. Men who worked for a wage, worked hard, but men who worked for freedom, worked with blind passion. Together, they believed they stood a chance.

Revenge motivated them as well. The men would confront the cartel in the names of all the innocent women who had been raped and beheaded. For all the shattered, starved families who could never be whole again, they would persevere. They would fight for those who had been hanged or kidnapped as payment of gang imposed taxes. Perhaps they would make history, be remembered and honored as martyrs should they die fighting. They would live with a hero's pride if they were successful. There was nothing to lose and all to gain.

Inside the trucks were suffocatingly hot and crowded. The lack of space left legs cramped and painful. The canvas had to remain closed so as not to attract attention to the live cargo, pretending to be sick with the Fever, until the border guards let them pass or not. They would even have to remain enclosed once the truck was speeding across the dusty familiar roads of their homeland. They needed to stay out of sight and unnoticed. The element of surprise was just as key to their success as being armed was.

The two trucks rumbled loudly at the border crossing while smoke spewed from the tail pipes. With Papi and Miguel behind the wheel, they waited, one truck behind the other in traffic. Santino usually alerted the border guards, who were hungry for bribes, to look out for his men when crossing. Papi recognized many, who also knew Papi's face, and hoped that these corrupted agents would focus solely on the bribe, forgetting that no call had been placed. Finally, the two trucks were waved over by a guard pointing off to one side to the place where trucks were being searched.

An agent approached the truck in front which Papi was driving. They exchanged a few words and the agent stepped around to the rear of the truck. Pulling the canvas hatch back, stale air poured over him, making him cough. At arm's length, he peered into the truck and saw men squatting and laying across other men. Papi had instructed his cargo to look as though they were truly sick and it wasn't difficult after riding in such cramped quarters for so long. The guard let the canvas fall from his hand after the first man coughed weakly and another moaned. Migrant workers returning to México weren't seen as much of a concern.

The guard returned to Papi for his bribe, a large bag of cocaine, and waved both trucks through. The stowaways were relieved, hugging each other while muttering, "Viva México," as they shifted around for space. The canvas could finally be lifted a bit on all sides and the back hatch flapped as they drove. The trip became slightly less ghastly from that point; the trucks cooled down as darkness fell and provided a curtain of protection.

The Fever, as it was known, had no medical explanation other than being identified as a virus with no treatment, therefore it was dreaded. It came without warning, and in spite of many attempts to save its victims, no one had survived thus far. It crept in like a thief and snatched its target's consciousness first and then laid waste to the person, in record time.

People in the farming community had been struck the worst, and though it could run through a farm like locusts, some were immune. Or, at least they seemed to be. The Fever didn't appear to be airborne though random cases did crop up. It should have been an epidemic, but the virus came in waves and then receded with the same fluid movement. A hospital stay could lengthen the life of someone who had contracted it, but when left to run its course on its own, the Fever only needed two days to stake its claim.

Papi had explained to the border agent that a few of the migrant workers in the trucks were showing signs of illness, possibly the Fever, so he had packed 'em up and was sending them back to México before the CDC could hear about it. He couldn't afford to have an outbreak of the Fever at the farm. The guard understood and was glad to be rid of Papi and his cargo.

***

Once the men were unloaded in Esperanza, they fanned out across town. In hushed voices, local merchants were told where to go to become part of the resistance and claim their weapons. These people had been regularly harassed by the cartel for tax money, so it was critical to weaponize these folks first. While attempting to stay out of sight, Miguel had chosen an abandoned home, nicely tucked under the cover of trees and low brush as a temporary station. He planned to move around though making an ambush more difficult.

Miguel felt that it would be easier to know who was truly ready to fight the cartels by inviting them into the resistance organization. "They should come to us, giving us a chance to make eye contact with them, make them feel part of the team. They will begin to bond as soldiers do, make that unbreakable attachment that endows a man with valor."

He knew that the first to arrive would be the most committed, needing little encouragement or supervision. The next to present themselves were either too engaged in running their businesses or too cursed with fear. The fearful men could be dangerous men; these men would need little encouragement to betray the resistance. The last to arrive had either taken time to expose the resistance; hoping for dispensation by the cartels, or taken the time to pray and brood over the knowledge of what they were about to do. No longer innocent in the eyes of God, they would have prayed to be forgiven. Miguel and the others spent more time with both of these last groups of men.

Handing out weapons took longer than he had hoped. A few men had to be taught how to shoot and clean their weapon; some had painful stories to share like confessions. These men hoped to be absolved of sin, to feel justified in their plans to switch from being the hunted to the hunter. Miguel was careful when he spoke, but he advised the volunteers that they were committing to the right side.

Some wanted shotguns. These guns discharge shrapnel, making the probability of missing an intended target unlikely. Others didn't have a place to keep a large gun and needed something smaller.

Women came too. Some needed lessons, hating the power and the sound of the guns, but others were more fearless than the men. This characteristic had been innate throughout history in México, but these women were the few who knew their cartel-controlled fate would be unendurable, so kill-or-be-killed was their motto. They were glad to have a fighting chance.

It had taken a long many days laying down the initial groundwork and all needed to rest. Santino was scheduled to travel in a few hours. They had to be ready.

7

The War

"Something is wrong," Gabriella hissed into the phone. "Santino is coming back. The others are continuing on, but he is coming back. I'm scared."

"Ok. Stay calm. We'll figure it out. Just stay put and act like nothing is wrong. There is no way you can be associated with what happens in the streets tonight."

She could hear Santino's shoes clicking on the floor of the hallway as he slowly approached her room. She was sure he was deliberately trying to cause her anxiety to build. He didn't come to her room often, so she could sense that something was wrong. The handle turned, and the door slowly swung open wide. Gabriella felt exposed. Santino stood for a moment in the doorway and then leaned against it; he crossed his arms, folding one foot over the other. He had never waited at the door before. Neither of them spoke.

Typically when Santino darkened her doorway, he would close the door and lock it. He would throw her a hateful glance and head for the shower, always without a word. Gabriella would cut him a couple lines, pour him a shot of whiskey from the lead crystal decanter and pull back his chair. After she hung his robe in the bathroom, she would freshen herself up as quickly as she could and wait.

Things would go better if she watched him move around the room after his shower. He enjoyed the attention and feeling in total control of her. If she looked away or turned her back on him, his belt would come off, and he would beat her. Either way, sex was imminent.

Santino would sit in the chair she had pulled back for him. After snorting a line or two, he would take a drink of the whiskey, and finally he would lean back. He would tip his head and run his fingers through his wet hair. He loved the touch of his own wet hair. Then he would inescapably and relentlessly turn his lustful attention toward Gabriella.

He came to Gabriella's room to strip of her dignity, always leaving her naked and feeling like a used rag doll. Santino liked to remind her of his power over her and then he would leave without a word. She had assumed that he felt it was beneath him to speak to her. She had never understood the source of his hatred for her, or why he continued to keep her in this house for himself.

The other girls spoke about Santino's visits as if they were parties. He would call for two or three at a time; they all would get high, laugh and eat. The girls said it wasn't too bad really because they had each other to giggle with. "He sometimes would get mean but mostly, it was easy work."

This night, Santino stood in the doorway brooding, his narrowed eyes and flared nostrils indicators of his contempt. Gabriella gathered her courage to speak, "I thought you were away tonight." He was surprised to hear her voice and flew at her, striking her across her face.

"Who said you could speak to me? I'll tell you if you can talk." Santino growled. "You thought… You thought I was away tonight? How would you know if I were here or away? What business is it of yours when I come and when I go? He bumped into her chair intentionally as he passed her. She sat with her hands folded in her lap fearful of his next hit. She couldn't see him behind her, so she nervously stood up and slowly began the ritual.

First, Gabriella readied the powder. Santino's threatening demeanor and cruel expression sent a shutter up her spine. As she reached for the whiskey, she felt Miguel's cell phone vibrate silently in the pocket of her jeans. Flinching, the bottle almost dropped and she spilled some. He crossed his arms again and said darkly, "You are nervous tonight." Gabriella didn't answer but kept her eyes on him. "Answer me!" he shouted.

Gabriella jumped, "I guess I am used to things going a certain way."

"I am used to things going a certain way, too." Santino snarled through gritted teeth. "I usually provide drugs to grateful people, and those people in turn provide money to me. But, that didn't happen!" He began to shout. "I did not get my money today! Where is Miguel, Gabriella? Hhmm? Where is he? This was his deal."

"I don't know anything about Miguel. I mean… I… I know that he had begun to work for you. Well, I assumed this when Maria went to stay with him in the states, but that's all I know."

"He hasn't tried to meet you?" Santino asked with a sneer. "He hasn't climbed through your window to see you? I find it hard to believe that he hasn't tried to contact you. Are you disappointed? Maybe he never loved you."

Gabriella's hands trembled openly now. It was hard for her to concentrate with the vibrating cell phone in her pocket. It felt bigger and heavier; it seemed to expand with her fear. She was sure Santino would notice it. She had hoped for a chance to hide it, but Santino hadn't taken his eyes off of her. She poured his drink, splashing whiskey onto the table. She quickly put the bottle down and sat.

Terror filler her as he strode toward her and stood over her. Gabriella gripped the arms of the chair as Santino filled his fist with her hair. He pulled her head back so she had no choice but to look at him. He slowly brought his face down to hers until his eyes glared in front of hers. He muttered through clenched teeth, "You look old, you ugly bitch. I should kill you just for being so ugly, never mind for lying to me." He spat on Gabriella's face and smiled as he watched the spittle drip down her check. Releasing her suddenly, Santino walked to the bathroom. She finally drew a full breath.

Once Gabriella heard the shower water flowing, she looked at the phone, reading a text message from Miguel. "We have five SUV's." She hid the phone out of sight.

Gabriella had often considered ways to kill Santino but had not followed through on any because she knew she had no means to escape afterward. Panic was setting in and all she was able to do was freeze and then pace and then panic. It was hard to think. Remembering the robe, she hastily placed it in the bathroom. The wet shower area was slippery. She didn't dare try anything there, so she walked out of the bathroom without washing up as he required. She had to find a way to kill Santino, but her mind froze. Nothing seemed right and he was certainly too strong for her.

Santino emerged from of the bathroom, and as usual, had washed some of his tension away. Preoccupied with thoughts of lost money, he collapsed into his chair with no complaint that she had not pulled it out for him. He made no protest to her standing, nervously fidgeting, by the table. As he bent his head to snort his first line, she grasped the whiskey decanter from the table and spun around, slamming it forcefully into his temple. She knew this strike to his temple would scramble his brain. Confused, he tipped to one side, righted himself, and with splayed fingers grabbed at his head, while attempting to stand. Gabriella reached up as he slowly stood, gripping Stantino's still damp hair in both her fists, she pulled with her full weight and slammed his head into the cocaine laden table top. Santino slid, cursing, to the floor. With all the strength she could muster, Gabriella tried to break his neck with a twist, but wasn't strong enough. She slammed the sharp edged heel of her shoe into his neck. His moaning stopped. She did this again twice more. She was in a fit.

Footsteps fell in the hallway outside her room. Gabriella looked up to see that Santino had left the door open as two guards ran in, one raised his weapon to her. She covered her face in fear. The shot that rang out was deafening. Gabriella screamed, stumbled and fell to the floor. She could hear herself breathing, but she was not able to move or open her eyes. Steps came toward her and she braced herself, but it was a tender hand that touched her arm. A voice asked, "Are you all right?" Frankie was at her side. Behind him, she caught a glimpse of the other guard, soaking in a pool of his own blood.

Her arms flew around Frankie's neck as Gabriella let out a sob. He said, "It's going to be all right. We have to get you out of here. We can figure out what's next." She shook her head in agreement and relief. Frankie checked his former boss for a pulse as he lay lifeless and askew, Santino's pulse was not detectable. His heart had failed when she severed his spinal cord. Gabriella gagged as she liberated the dead guard of his weapon, taking his extra clips, money and keys as well, stuffing these into a large packed handbag as she removed it from the closet. She placed the phone and charger in it as well.

Though it was difficult for her to touch him, together they shoved Santino under the bed, out of sight. Frankie shut and locked the door as they walked out. He smiled, turning to Gabriella he said, "You have always been able to surprise me." For many years Frankie's job had been guarding against Gabriella's escape, but she had always thought of Frankie as a protector as well, a father figure who had often been kind to her. With him by Gabriella's side she was able to think more clearly again. She explained to

Frankie that Miguel had organized a large resistance group and tonight they were about to rescue the abducted kids.

Gabriella called Miguel on the cell phone. "Miguel, I killed him. Santino's dead. I am with Frankie, one of his guards. He says he will help if he can. Miguel, Frankie says there are land mines surrounding the building where the kids are being held. One will set off the next and the building will collapse on those kids. Frankie wants to meet you there. We will be making a stop first, but we will meet you there."

***

The guards at the weapons bunker were surprised to see Frankie, but they welcomed him, casually asking him why he had stopped by. One guard handed his bottle of whiskey to Frankie and sat down as if to chat. Frankie said, "I just wanted to check things out. It's a strange night. Is everything okay down here?" They each drank from the bottle. One guard spotted Gabriella in the car parked at a distance and asked, "Who's your friend?" Frankie answered with a bullet to his head and then he shot the others too.

Gabriella helped load what they could into Frankie's SUV. Filling the space quickly, there was a great deal they would have to leave behind. She grabbed bullet-proof vests, night vision goggles, gas masks, surveillance equipment, Bluetooth ear buds, and infrared heat sensors. She was thinking defensively. Frankie loaded piles of ammunition, semi-automatic rifles, hand grenades, and a short-range missile at the last. Both watched the other with surprise as they made their hurried selections.

"This is a great way to get to know a person." Frankie offered with a grin.

"But, I didn't know what a short-range missile looked like until this very minute. I might have picked that." They both laughed nervously. The excitement of this evening was almost overwhelming.

***

Sharkie had instructed Miguel to pinch off the fuel hoses on the SUV's at the club. The vehicles would start but run out of gas just outside of the parking lot, out of sight. The plan had worked perfectly. Miguel had men waiting in the scrub; when a driver got out to figure out what had happened to his engine, he was shot dead.

It was harder to shoot the men still inside the trucks as they struggled to organize their drug induced thoughts and locate their fire arms. The panic in their eyes demonstrated their want to survive making it difficult to destroy them at point blank range.

Miguel had warned his men that this might happen, telling them to hold an image of a lost loved one in their minds in order to fire. Each was shot in the heart minimizing the suffering as well as bloody mess, and it was done. The cars were emptied of their lifeless, forlorn inhabitants who were swiftly dragged into the brush.

***

The night club had cleared out, as usual, and Maria began working to undo the drunken damage the guests had caused. The place closed when the last of its customers left. After all, management had little regard for the working girls so as long as money might be made, they stayed open for business. There were always stragglers, and tonight was no different. Marcos, usually accompanied by a pair of friends, were often some of them.

Marcos was a beer drinker who worked pretty hard early each evening to prove it, but by the end of the night he usually sobered up, becoming clearheaded once again. His buddies, however, drank like they were deliberately trying to forget something, relenting only when they could barely raise their own drinks to their mouths. They always thought it was funny to watch each other trying.

Marcos would lose interest in them and begin moving around the club on his own. He would peer around corners to see what newly formed couple had discovered kissing to be a suddenly irresistible pass-time. He tried on sunglasses left behind at a table. He would check the parking lot for trouble and occasionally he even brought his used glasses to the bar where the dishwasher was, the dishwasher that Maria filled each evening.

Maria had been warned that something was going to happen on this night, so when Marcos meandered toward the door, she thought it best to stop him. A large group of cartel elders had left shortly before; it was best to keep him from stumbling onto a scene where he might interfere.

"How about bringing a few of those glasses up here?" Maria's figure had transformed into that of a woman, whether she liked it or not, but her voice still had the delicacy of a child. Marcos turned his head in surprise, and then doubled back to collect some glasses.

Maria wished her voice had not wavered. She had hoped to speak with authority. If she had spoken boldly, Marcos would have brought the glasses to her, and that would be the end of it. But the sweetness in her voice sounded, even to her, like a girl who wanted to have an excuse to talk to a boy. Instantly, she had regret.

Marcos' confused expression turned to one of curiosity as he approached Maria at the bar. He placed the glasses down, and she quietly thanked him. He held onto of one glass as she attempted to take it from him. He wore a playful smile; Maria shyly smiled back when she realized it was a game.

She had gotten Marcos's attention as intended and was pretty sure he would stay at the bar a while, but she couldn't encourage him any further. Needing an excuse to get away from him, she noticed two men still sitting at a nearby booth and pretended that they had ordered another round. She carried the drinks over to them herself.

"We are supposed to bring you with us when you can break away. We will be waiting here for the right time," one said as she place their drinks on the table. Maria was startled and stepped back as she drew a breath.

"Everything all right over there?" Marcos asked. This was more of a directive than a question. What he implied was that everything had better be all right over there. Maria returned to the bar.

"What happened?" he asked.

"Nothing. I thought I saw a mouse."

"Really? A mouse?" Marcos said, laughing. "A mouse is gonna scare a girl like you? Don't try to tell me you've never seen a mouse before, especially considering where you live." He quickly realized how harsh he sounded. "I'm sorry. I just meant that…"

"It's no big deal. Let it go," Maria intentionally sounded irritated. She hoped he would stop talking to her.

"That's enough, Marcos. It's getting late. You should think about heading out soon, don't you think?" said Jazmin, the club supervisor who had noticed Maria's discomfort. Jazmin kept everyone in line; customers, Santino's men and the girls. She hadn't fired her weapon at anyone in a long time, but she was known to possess a twitchy trigger finger and deadly accuracy.

Marcos arose from the bar and began wandering again. Eventually boredom set in, and he left. Maria kept her distance from the men in the booth until she checked her cell phone and saw a text from her mother's phone that read, "You can trust them. Get away when you can."

8

The Captives

Miguel and the others met with Frankie as he led the way to the cement building where Santino kept the children. Three guards were perched outside the grey, windowless cell room. There were two narrow openings in the front of the building, but no doors to close or lock.

The first guard stood up when the SUV's approached, carefully aiming his rifle at a single point on the ground only ten feet from his boots. Miguel understood that his target was a land mine, and everyone would be killed with a single quiver of the guard's finger.

Miguel and Frankie got out of the cars, but Gabriella had stayed seated. Miguel had not had an opportunity to look at her. She remained still, observing him move. She watched the intensity of his expression and saw intelligence in his eyes. He had grown into a handsome man. Her heart responded even in this dark gloomy place.

Miguel took aim at the guard but would be unable to shoot until the guard shifted away from the targeted land mine. He was patient and the heavy gun was not a burden to him. He had spent long parts of his day holding this exact pose only a month before, when he was still an enlisted man. Miguel waited while Frankie spoke.

"Listen to me," Frankie pleaded. "Don't shoot. *Amigo*, Santino is dead. Everyone is dead. The townspeople are armed and ready to fight. All we want is to free the children tonight. You can be free, too, if you help us. The cartel is fractured. The resistance is a strong united force, willing to die in this fight to regain their dignity. And this, what you are doing here, is wrong. Can you remember back to a time when your own mother was proud of you? Claim your self-respect man and put down the weapon. You don't have to die tonight."

The guard turned slightly to see the faces of the other two. They looked like men who were choosing to live. Miguel saw his opportunity as the guard's sights had changed when his shoulders turned, and he fired. The gun dropped from the guard's wounded hand, and all three men carefully raised their arms high in the air. Frankie spoke first, "Good decision, *amigos*. Now, walk toward me. Show me the path we need walk to peace and freedom."

The front doorway was nothing more than two separate slot openings. A normal sized person could fit through one shoulder at a time, a foreboding of what lay inside. Anxiety tugged at stomachs as they tried to comprehend the reason for the lack of security and a front entrance without a locking door.

The three guards warned Miguel and his group of what to expect inside, but there was no way to emotionally prepare for it. Two of Miguel's men remained outside in case of trouble, but one by one they followed the path to the building and disappeared through the slot, where sorrow became inescapable and permanent.

The walls within were lined with four-foot long, four-foot wide, four-foot high wooden boxes, inside of which a precious child was imprisoned. The bottom of each box was constructed of wire, which allowed feces and urine to drop into the pan below. There was a small hole in the front through which food or water might have been passed. Before they could see into the room, Miguel and his men had to pause near the doorway, choking and gagging from the rancid odor that filled the place. They covered their noses and mouths with their arms and blinked until their now watering eyes adjusted to the dim light.

In the back of the room, with a light hanging above, stood a blood-stained table, surgical tools placed around it. Beverage coolers lined the wall. Chains with ankle cuffs were anchored to the floor where the children would wait for the cages to be constructed or for the organs to be removed. It was hard to register such a foreign scene.

One guard instructed Miguel's men to begin at the left front of the room, as those children were the newest deliveries and more likely to be alive. He said matter-of-factly that some die of the Fever, some children suffocate from the toxicity of the air, some starve or just die of stress. Miguel punched him in the face. The guard didn't fight back. He looked ashamed.

Because the boxes were twice the width of the doorway, they had to check each, one at a time, while in the putrid room. The guards had bandanas to cover their noses, and several gas masks were given to those who ventured deeper in to the room.

Miguel turned the latch on one of the boxes and pulled the first door open. A deep, guttural inhuman sound escaped him. He quickly closed the door and braced himself against it. Gabriella suddenly appeared at his side. "Together," she said. "We will do it together." She clasped Miguel's hand tightly.

Miguel unlatched the doors, opened them wide and moved on without looking in. Gabriella glanced in quickly, making the declaration and closing each door. "Dead.... dead.... dead..." The sights inside these boxes was so gruesome, she was overcome as well, and their pace slowed. Gabriella needed to recover in between, stifling a sob at each door and quietly announcing "dead."

Of the fifty boxes in the cell-room, twenty-five children were still alive. These dirty, slightly conscious and weak were loaded into SUVs and were driven to Frankie's house. Frankie had told Miguel's men to look for a path with an unlit light post. "Follow that path, and you will find a basement door. It is blocked off from the rest of the house, but it has medical supplies, water and blankets." Frankie's wife would be home, but she would not acknowledge them. With Padre Cayo's help, he had been hiding girls there whenever he could for years.

An overwhelming sadness befell the group. There were no words to describe a tragedy such as this. It was beyond the comprehension of a normal mind. One at a time, the rescuers were overcome; their strength fleeing them as they stood in the night air. Each fell back against an SUV, sliding down to sit or crouch on the dirt. Tears didn't come; their lungs barely opened to allow air to flow. This place had to be hell itself.

"The human race is the single worst thing that could have ever happened to this planet," Miguel said to no one. "Human beings are the only species that kills for the sport of it with no respect for what God has created. This place violates what it is to be human."

Their hearts mourned for the children, for the suffering, the needless, endless torment. Their hearts ached for the parents. They felt despair for the community, for the pride of México.

"Miguel, we have to go to the police." Gabriella insisted. "We have to give these kids and their families some peace."

"I can't leave them. I can't get up. I can't turn my back and leave them here, alone." Miguel said.

Frankie encouraged Miguel with a pat on the shoulder. "No more harm can come to them and there is still so much work left to do."

***

The plan was going well so far. It seemed that they had not been detected yet. When morning came and husbands did not return from the club, the real trouble would begin. For the moment, everyone could take a break and reorganize. At some point, someone at Santino's house would get suspicious and look for him. Time would be running out.

At the police station, three leathery-looking men filled in around Miguel and Gabriella. One sat at the table with them while the other two propped themselves against the wall. One officer asked, "What is that foul sink? You stink. How can you come in here this way?"

Miguel said pointedly, "It is the smell of death, from the Gates of Hell. A place so horrible the devil himself wouldn't go there."

Miguel was there to report a terrible crime, but quickly discerned that he was being interrogated. These officers had clearly worked for Santino; they were on his payroll. Miguel had been aware of that before he entered the police station and knew it was dangerous to be there, but this had to be dealt with. Parents needed to be located and remains buried respectfully.

Miguel showed the seated officer a photo on his phone, which had been taken by a member of the resistance. Displaying the small cages; it demonstrated the horror. The first image was of a partially decomposed seven year-old girl, awkwardly splayed across a cage floor with a bloody, poorly stitched incision. Fecal matter and dried urine stained the cage floor beneath the wire where her starved frame was sprawled. The little hand closest to the camera looked normal in sharp contrast. It looked as though it was reaching out to them.

The officer's stomach turned sour and expelled its contents with violent force. The other two turned away, unable to look at it. "Now who stinks?" Miguel asked. "Do you have children, officers?" They began taking Miguel's report.

Miguel stated that Santino was dead, as were many of the heads of families, but didn't reveal how he knew. The officer behaved angrily until he began to understand that the cartel had been splintered. It was interesting to watch his face as his allegiance changed. The officer would suffer no adverse consequences right now if he finally did his job. Miguel thought the officer had begun to sound as if he wanted to cooperate.

Miguel focused on the need to change things. He scolded the officers, saying that they needed to do their jobs as law enforcement from now on. "No one else needs to die. We don't care about drugs. We only want the raids to stop and the children to be freed. Mexicans want to come home, to be proud again, but they need to be safe."

An officer stood up and left the room. Miguel knew he would begin calling around to verify if Santino was really dead. Bedlam would not be avoided after this call. Miguel saw this as their cue to leave while they were still able to. The other two officers attempted to stop them, but Gabriella pulled out a small handgun, saying, "I welcome you to take your chances here boys, or we can all go home for the night. You'll know where to find us in the morning."

***

While Gabriella and Miguel were meeting with the police, and others were caring for the children at Frankie's, a third group of six men had been assigned the task of blowing up one of the meth tents. It was an important step. The cartel needed to understand that the resistance could match their ruthlessness, and Miguel felt that the continued threat of financial loss might encourage cooperation.

The tent was an hours drive south from the Gates of Hell, hidden behind a small hill. All that was needed was to fire a short-range missile into it and watch the fireball mushroom. Never has a coup be armed before so well. Their good fortune would make all the difference.

Two men exited the car and quietly climbed the gentle slope. Once the target was identified, they launched one missile. A thunderous explosion rang out and an inferno grew, flames reaching into the night sky like flailing, fiery arms. The two men paused, captivated by the sensational blaze. From the car, the others watched the silhouette of their comrades on the hill. At first they stood still, but then began to jerk and twist, finally falling to the ground. The men guarding the tent had begun shooting. Startled out of their trance, the others sped away with bullets crashing through the glass windows of their SUV. They headed south, abandoning their fallen comrades on the incline without knowing if they were dead or alive. Their confidence quickly abated.

For these men, heading south was "going home," where their job was to find and organize another group of men and women and arm them against the neighboring cartel. They had hoped to share the story of their success, but the glory of their victory was left behind with their fallen friends. A terrifying reminder that poking at a sleeping dragon usually leaves burns.

***

A thousand acres of plant life were chemically devastated in that one night. The effect would last for years to come; it was the perfect finishing touch. No could have expected it. At first light field guards were dozing at their posts, a wooden fort-like structure built high up on stilts, when the two planes flown by Papi and Ben roared across the fields in front of them. This was their final pass. One guard said, "Hey! When did we start crop dusting? Shit. That stuff is poisonous to breath. They should have warned us that they were dusting today."

The other peered out from under the hat covering his face and said, "Relax, something's eventually gonna get you. How bad can the stuff be?"

"Are you seriously asking me that? Don't you read, you ignorant fuck? That shit is mutating the bugs and bacteria and stuff. They think that the bacteria living on these plants mutate into something else when you spray them. They think those chemicals are causing the Fever. And, that's why they can't cure it. It's not natural. They call 'em super bugs or something."

"Scary. Watch out for those super bugs and the global warming too. Idiot! Are you afraid of the monsters under your bed, you gullible chump?"

A couple of hours later, when the shift change arrived, the plants were already beginning to wilt.

***

The explosion at the meth tent set off a chain reaction of phone calls. It was at about that time that someone finally discovered a substantial puddle of blood and the expired guard along with Santino, who had been tucked under Gabriella's bed. When the men from the club hadn't returned home, a search party found them that morning scattered just beyond the tree line at the club. Their bodies had been arranged in a design that formed the words, "Viva México."

***

Frankie had volunteered to pick up Maria, who had been kept safe and out of the way by the men who collected her from the club. It was a great help to Miguel and Gabriela who were completely spent and not certain they could keep Maria safe. Frankie he was still able to move around freely, no one knew yet that he had been aiding the resistance. He planned to bring Maria to Miguel and Gabriella after doing a bit of recon. It would be helpful to know the extent of the night's damage. What he learned was deeply saddening.

The cartel owned a hierarchy of snitches and informants. They were the first confronted by the cartel's henchmen who were expecting to hear and explanation for the nights events. Many were found hanging from bridges at sunrise, resembling piñatas as they dangled in their designer jeans, swaying in the breeze. The victims looked the same as in life, with hair flowing and their curves showing youth or old age.

It was hard to know if the cartel had learned anything from these people before hanging them. In Frankie's experience, people always had to pay for a slight to the cartel. It didn't always have to be the offending party. The cartel at times exercised patience, but sometimes, as in this instance, they just lashed out.

Worse than swinging from a bridge was not knowing the fate of those whom the gangs had kidnapped. Frankie had been told that several townspeople had vanished randomly. It was worse to not know if a loved one was suffering than it was to see them in front of you, dead or alive. In the past it had been said that the gunmen would shoot hostages once to impair them so they are not able to get away, and then they would bury them alive.

The townspeople had been warned this attack would come when they had been given their weapons. Most had learned how to shoot rifles as young boys and girls, but M16s and the like were foreign and challenging to use. Several SUVs had been burned and left on the roadside, victims still seated inside, a sign that those who the resistance had armed, fought well.

The rumor Frankie overheard was that cartelistas finally withdrew when they discovered that hundreds of townspeople had been armed with semi-automatic rifles and grenades. Things settled down, becoming eerily calm. Since the fight from the resistance side was completed and with nothing to protect immediately, each side had time to assess the damage and regroup. Santino's replacement had to be assigned, and bodies had to be mourned and then buried.

***

Gabriella and Miguel drove in silence. It was a comfortable silence. So much had happened the day before, and they both needed to process it. Miguel had longed to see his childhood home and took advantage of the cessation to visit it.

Miguel was relieved to see that the structure, the bones of his childhood home, had held. His family's old house looked as he remembered it, though it seemed smaller. Debris that had been carried in by the wind was scattered through the yard; only weeds flourished in his mothers' garden. This was the first time he had ever seen the property without flowers in bloom.

"What's wrong, Miguel." Gabriella asked.

"I don't know. It doesn't feel right."

"What do you mean?"

"It doesn't feel like my home. I mean, I remember it, but now it's just a building." Miguel said, "It's so dark inside. It looks as though it died when we left Esperanza, when my mother died in the desert. I had thought that returning to this house was what I needed to heal, but now I think I was wrong. I don't know if this house can ever feel like home again. I didn't know that until this moment."

"I'm sorry, Miguel. Maybe we should go inside." Gabriella urged. "Let's try to remember it the way it was."

"It looks so small," he laughed as he said it.

Once inside, Miguel drew a breath and remembered the smell of it. Every house has a distinct fragrance and he had loved the scent of his. The two of them moved through the rooms, side by side, remembering things from adolescence. They talked about the games they had played and the meals they had eaten. They remembered studying at *Abuela's* dining room table, or under it, as both happened frequently. They exchanged smiles and quiet laughter. Being home was beginning to feel better.

A photo of Miguel's family, his complete family, stared back at him from a shelf in front of him, taking Miguel by surprise. He had been a family of two for as long as he had been a family of four, and now he was forced to remember them—his mother and brother. Miguel broke down and wept has he ran his fingers across their images. It had been so long since he had seen his mother's face; he had barely remembered her features until he saw this photo. It was difficult to look at his little brother's eyes; he was so young and full of life in the photo, but he had barely even had a chance to live.

Gabriella and Miguel had not slept at all the night before. Exhaustion overwhelmed them and they fell asleep on a dusty couch with photo books scattered around them. The church bells that rang for nine o'clock Mass were always a signal that all was well. They wouldn't be awake to hear them ring in only a few hours.

***

The song of the church bells was *Abuela's* favorite sound in the world. All her life, no matter what she was doing when they sounded, she would stop, listen and say a little grateful prayer. As a child, a feeling that all was well would wash over her when the church bells rang. She still felt that way today. To her, they symbolized God's love, and *Abuela* was always happy for the reminder. The old stone church comforted her since childhood too and now she was glad to be serving as Deacon there. She missed spending time with her dear, old friend, Padre Cayo, though.

"The Executioner" served Morning Mass as usual to a small group of parishioners who needed to feel a connection with God more than they needed to elude this vile person. This morning, the morning after the resistance had struck, the parishioners formed a short line to make their confessions, and *Abuela* watched, standing quietly off to one side.

As the last parishioner exited, she entered the confessional box and said, "Forgive me Padre… for you have sinned."

"The Executioner" hissed, "Get out of my confessional old woman. You don't even know the right thing to say to me."

"I said it right, Padre. You have sinned, Padre. Forgive me." She lifted her clasped hands to the screen through which his shadow-like profile lurked, and fired. "The Executioner" fell to the floor with a thud.

With ears buzzing from the gun's reverberation, *Abuela* dialed Padre Cayo's number, one digit at a time. She couldn't hear it ring, and she couldn't hear him answer, so she decided to simply say what she wanted him to know.

"Padre, you need to come to church. The priest that replaced you has left a big mess. You need to come to the church to help clean up his mess. I can't hear you. You need to come to the church right now."

Abuela waited for Padre and prayed. She cried tears of relief that "The Executioner" would never hurt another child. She prayed that Miguel and Papi were safe and that the captive children were alive and well. She prayed that she would soon see her grandson and Gabriella, together once again.

Hours passed with Abuela longing for Padre Cayo to arrive, calling him again and again. She came to realize that her hearing would not return. She had sacrificed her ability to listen to the lovely church bells when she fired that one shot inside the small confessional. As she prayed, she told God that she had no regrets and she would do it again if given the choice. Firing that one shot had provided her more peace than hearing the bells had ever given. She assured God that she would remember their sound and the way they had made her feel. That was something she would never lose.

9

The Mayor

After a few short hours of restless sleep, Miguel left Gabriella to look for the Mayor, finding the nervous, distracted man in his office. Miguel showed him the pictures of the dead, mutilated children from his phone and explained that a rebel group had been formed and armed. Miguel was pleased with the powerful effect the photos were having on the Mayor. He was clearly upset and disgusted.

"The first priority is to get these kids to a hospital and then back to their families, if they have families. We need to be sure they will be safe, so we need government support. That is not negotiable. It won't be easy to find their families, but it will be easy to find out which towns the cartels have recently raided. That's a start."

The mayor's office was nicely appointed with luxurious fabric and hand carved mahogany furniture. Law books lined the back wall where an antique silver tea set was carefully placed beside to a crystal whiskey decanter and some artifacts from Aztec period of México's history.

Most often in a middle class town like this one, the mayor's office would be located in the same building as the police station, the courtroom and a small jail. Esperanza was no exception. At the end of the street, towering grandly over everything like a watchful parent, was the Catholic Church.

The mayor's office phone rang constantly. He would look at the phone but not answer it. He seemed relieved when the ringing stopped and tense up when it started again. It was hard to know who he was avoiding, but Miguel was certain that the mayor wouldn't be taking calls as long as he was in the office, where he couldn't be sure who was listening in.

"The government should not attempt to suppress the resistance," Miguel explained with authority that he hadn't yet earned. "But instead, you must work with this rebel group to stop the terror of the cartels." The mayor didn't have to explain that he feared for his life. He was clearly at a point near frenzy, frantically pacing the office but never too near the windows. Miguel hoped to make the mayor believe that if Miguel were crazy enough to execute his coup to this point, he would stop at nothing.

The mayor said that vigilantly groups were illegal and could not be allowed. Miguel explained that murder, kidnapping and rape cannot be allowed, adding that Santino was dead, as well as the other heads of families. No emotion registered in the mayor's face. Clearly Miguel was telling him what he already knew. "The crops are dead. Now we have a good place from which to build. The war has begun. Be on the right side."

Miguel explained that he would be speaking to the people of Esperanza in the morning at the marketplace, and that the mayor should be there. Miguel expected protection from any police or military who might attend. The mayor made no promises; he just kept running his fingers through the hair at his temples down to his neck. Miguel warned that the resistance would be there too. He didn't mention that Gabriella would have already spread the word to the local and American media. The element of surprise on this point might just save his life.

Miguel effectively placed a target on his back by talking so openly with the mayor. The cartel would be able to focus their retaliation on him. He had already decided that he, Gabriella and Maria should not sleep in the same place more than one night at a time. Miguel worried about Gabriella especially. Santino had kept her captive for years as a means of controlling him, and he was sure that they would attempt to use her again. He decided that they might have to split up. He wondered if Maria knew how to fire a gun.

***

Based on Miguel's military training and Frankie's intimate understanding of the cartel, it was obvious that the cartelistas could easily toss one grenade or fire one short range missile at the house and the game would be over in a fiery minute. But, it was more likely that they would try to approach the house and terrorize its occupants before killing them. They decided to remain at Miguel's for another night for lack of another plan. They were all exhausted and being in familiar surroundings was a comfort. They made a rudimentary system for defending against an attack.

They estimated the distance between Miguel's house and the neighbors to determine which gun would be most accurate to reach that distance, if necessary. Frankie explained that a shooter would likely try to sidle up close to the house. He ran that distance so they would have an idea of how much time it would take their enemy to cross it. They lined the yard in tripwire, hoping to hear a predator better after stumbling. They collected and then scattered sticks, pine cones and bits of tin in order to make anyone approaching more easily heard. Furniture was pushed against external walls to slow an incoming bullet.

Miguel had placed a weapon at each window, and reviewed the firing method of each. Frankie, Miguel, and Gabriella took turns that first night, keeping watch through a set of night vision goggles. No one really rested, their sleep disturbed by what seemed like bad dreams but were actually flashbacks from the horrors of the previous day.

The resistance as a whole was resting, recruiting, fortifying their homes and preparing their families. Padre Cayo, with Abuela's help, tended to the children at Frankie's basement hideout and carefully transported them to the hospital. He couldn't allow anyone to find out about Frankie's house, so this was an exhausting assignment. Papi and Ben had made it back to Arizona and were spreading the word, to the Mexican-American population and the media that the resistance had staged a coup against Santino's cartel and the leader of the resistance movement would be speaking the following morning.

Miguel hated public speaking and seemed more nervous about making a statement in public than he had been about any of the recent events. Gabriella brushed at his shirt and straightened his collar. She was so close to him, and seemed to enjoy touching him; Miguel leaned down to kiss her lips. She pulled back instinctively, stammering, "I'm sorry Miguel. I don't know why I did that. Please be patient with me. I think I am going to have to learn how to be normal again. I'm sorry."

The last few days had been exhausting and full of emotion. Miguel hadn't really thought about kissing Gabriella; it just happened naturally. He still loved her. In that moment, Miguel reminded himself that Gabriella had been through a terrible time, and he had not even begun to learn about it.

"No. I'm the one who is sorry. I wasn't thinking." He didn't want to be thinking about the horrors Gabriella had endured. There was so much else to think about.

Miguel wondered if he would be shot in the middle of the marketplace. He wondered if people were so accustomed to being threatened and punished by the cartels, that they would not respond to him. Maybe they would all turn and just walk away. He didn't have a plan for that.

Frankie drove the three of them to the marketplace. Local camera crews and journalists had come from all around to hear what Miguel had to say. American reporters were there, too. The appearance and presence of the media made Miguel more nervous about speaking publicly, but they were insurance that he would likely live through this day.

Moving slowly through the crowd of thousands, people had begun to recognize Miguel and stepped aside, leaving a wide path in front of him. He could hear the sounds of familiar prayers being mumbled. Some reached out and touched his shoulder as he passed.

Reaching the fountain in the center of the marketplace, Miguel stood up on its base so that he was standing above the people. A hush fell over the crowd as he waited, glancing around at all of the businesses that lined the streets. They all looked as though frozen in time—frozen since his childhood. Many of the faces were familiar, too, but older. He looked for the mayor but didn't see him.

What had changed were the camera crews, but more importantly, the military presence and the armed resistance Miguel could clearly survey stationed around the marketplace. He couldn't see the pistols, rifles and semi-automatic weapons he had given the merchants, but he knew they were there as well. Miguel breathed in a deep cleansing breath and readied himself to speak. Gabriella handed him a microphone, and he began.

***

"Our President, Desiderio Juarez, promised us when we elected him that he would not turn a blind-eye to the damage the cartels have done to México's people. That was two years ago and things have only gotten worse.

What is the worth of a government when its people do not thrive? I ask you, could the people of México not achieve chaos and mayhem on their own?

Imagine a time without a governing entity. What is the worst that could happen to the Mexican people or even the human race?" Miguel stood with his arms spread wide as if embracing the entire community. *"This—this hollow, Godless existence, dominated by evil, is the worst thing that could happen to the human race; with or without a governing entity.*

I challenge the governors of México and President Desiderio Juarez, to stand together against evil. Remember why you chose to be revered as an example of greatness and leadership. Remember why you asked the people of México to allow you to be exemplary. You have let us down.

In the grand scheme of this life, each of us individually is nothing. Together, however, we can be great. Two nights ago was an example of people achieving great things together. Together we were strong enough to fight back against Santino and his murderous cartel. And, we will not stop until we all are safe.

Our community lost many daring people that night; we will continue to honor their memory and tell stories of their bravery. We were once the greatest society living on Earth. Together, with our governors, our God, our culture of humble, happy, grateful people, we can be the greatest nation again.

We must reclaim our culture. We must stand up against evil. America demands her drugs and we cannot stop her. We can, however, allow our fertile land to satisfy her cravings while feeding our people. Both purposes have co-existed before and they can exist together again... in peace.

We can no longer accept the brutality of the drug cartels. We, as a government and as a people, cannot permit murder, abductions, torture, the harvesting of innocent children's organs, rape, or taxation levied by individuals outside the government.

I do not know how to encourage you to be brave, as I know you have suffered enough. I do not believe that God's protection will be sufficient to shield you. The worst may be coming. Do whatever you can. Stand together for there is no place else to run. We must save ourselves and in doing so, save México.

Our resistance group is growing daily. We are armed and ready to die for the purpose of freeing our good people from the terror Santino's gangs have inflicted upon you.

To the cartels: No more taxation, no more abductions for unpaid taxes, no more murder, no more rape; and God forgive you, no more organ harvesting.

Re-join humanity. You have stepped too far from the warmth of God's light. He will welcome you back. Keep your money and reclaim your business as it was before this unholy power struggle. You will be remembered as legend in México if you search your hearts and find a way to thrive without turning away from God. We must do better than this. Viva México!"

The people stood in stunned silence. After several moments, someone in the crowd slowly began to clap their hands together and then another did the same. Suddenly, everyone was clapping and shouting, pumping their fists in the air. Tears of relief glistened on Miguel's face as the roar from the crowd went on and on. Miguel stepped down from the fountain, and the crowd pressed in on him. They all wanted to touch him and to be near him. He became engulfed by the crowd.

Gabriella turned toward Frankie, who had been standing by her side. She was surprised to find him gone. Gabriella held Maria's hand tightly as she jumped up and down with excitement and pride.

The focus had shifted away from Miguel as large deliveries of baked goods were distributed around the plaza. There was bread and chicken and beer. There were cookies and soft drinks. Mariachi bands began to play, and people began to dance as though it were a grand festival.

Miguel shook hands and talked with as many people as he could until Sharkie presented himself. "Where did all this food come from, Sharkie?"

Sharkie laughed, saying that the charge cards they had confiscated from the men they had killed at the club were still active, so he had used them. He said he had deliveries scheduled for the next three days. "The poorest areas will get new shoes, blankets, food, water purifiers and medicine," he said. "Your people will never forget this day or this speech." They shook hands while laughing and then embraced.

"Have you seen Frankie? I lost sight of him right after the speech."

"Nope. I have been watching Gabriella and Maria. As a matter of fact, I would like it if they were a little closer." He kept his eyes on the girls as he left Miguel, moving toward where they were celebrating beside the fountain. "Keep doing your thing. Make some new friends."

***

The next morning, Padre Cayo stopped by many homes. The community was emotionally damaged after living in fear for so long, people craved his moral support and guidance. Unfortunately many were now more fearful of what was to come. Padre found Gabriella and Maria with Miguel at his family home.

Padre Cayo asked for Miguel's confession and prayed with him first, then Maria approached him and to pray and finally, Gabriella. She took the longest.

Miguel, who was more comfortable when he was busy, found many projects in need of his attention. It was easier to think when he was working. He was expecting some fallout from his speech and from all the damage they had inflicted on the cartels. He contemplated the possibilities while he gathered his tools.

Miguel had become passionate about wanting to hoist the green, white and red Mexican flag once again in front of his childhood home. He chose the perfect place and began digging a hole for a new flagpole at the end of the walkway. Miguel heard the sound of an SUV approaching. He stood up, wiped the sweat from his brow and watched. He had his pistol with him and instinctively wanted to un-holster it and take aim. But, he waited.

The driver's face was hidden by pair of large reflective glasses and the shade cast by the roof of the car. His arm was draped down against the side of the SUV. Banging his hand on the side of the car several times, he motioned with two fingers from his eyes to Miguel. It meant that whoever this was, he was watching Miguel.

The boom of a gun shot rang out, and the driver's head shattered like a watermelon dropped on a sidewalk. Miguel was taken by surprise. He flinched and covered his head. Blood and brain covered the seats and glass. He looked back to the house to see Gabriella rising from her knee at the window to stand and said, "What the hell?"

Gabriella replied, "Why have bulletproof windows if you're not gonna use 'em?" and laughed.

Miguel's ears were ringing, "What?"

She came out and stood in front of him, "He's not watching you anymore," she said showing him a toothy grin.

Miguel said, "Do you know what post-traumatic stress disorder is? Well, you're giving it to me."

She laughed and dialed the cell phone he had given her, "Sharkie, I have another SUV that needs its VIN numbers scraped. Yes. Same thing. Upholstery is a mess too. Fine. I know it takes a ton of time. I know it's disgusting. Sure, we can sell this one."

Padre Cayo interjected as he came out of the house, joining them on the walk way, "The church is still in need."

Sharkie moaned into the phone, "But the next one is mine to sell for sure. Promise me Gabby." Gabriella promised.

"There is a place for you in heaven, Sharkie, my boy," Padre said as he leaned toward the cell phone mouthpiece. "There is a place for you in my pews on Sunday as well." Padre Cayo mocked.

"Ok. See you soon then, Sharkie." Gabriella added. "Oh. The trash will be in the back. Can you get rid of it for me? Yes, I know Sharkie. It's gonna cost."

"Miguel, I was with your *Abuela* a few hours ago." Pedre said, "She's well and though she is not in pain, she is as deaf as your father's horse in one ear." He watched both Gabriella and Miguel rubbing their ears as though it would stop the ringing. Padre added, "It would seem that the Garces family might be more careful around guns before you all become hard of hearing. Your grandmother is going to help me at the church, but right now she is spending time with the children who have been moved from Frankie's house to the hospital. She sends her love and wants to see you soon. You too, Gabriella." He waved as he climbed into his car.

As they watched Padre drive away, Miguel asked Gabriella, "So, what are we going to do? Just blow everyone's head off now?"

The smile fell off of Gabriella's face, "I know your life has been hard, Miguel. Damn hard. But, walk a mile in my shoes and see how you feel. Live the way I have for half your life, and you will understand. That piece of shit was just waiting for his orders before he shot us. He didn't drive past here for the scenic view. They're watching us. It is unfortunate that it was so easy for him to find us. I'm happy to have my dignity back, and I will not risk losing it again."

Miguel stepped forward and kissed his friend's forehead. "Fine. I get it. And, you're right. We still have to be vigilant because it is just a matter of time before Santino's gangs reorganize, plus other families will try to move in, too. I am hoping that we bought ourselves some time by devastating those thousand acres. Not much time, but toxic land isn't in demand until it can grow something other than corn and soybeans. We need a better plan. Power corrupts Gabriella. No one should have absolute power."

"Okay then. While you're working that out, I'll be shooting the fuckers. I am not sure you recognize the danger we are in. Aren't you a little surprised we are even alive? I am. Revenge is coming. You need to be ready. I love being home, being free. I will die before I exist in that half-life again."

10

Frankie

Everyone had a job. Miguel was meeting with politicians. Gabriella brought back stories from their men. Padre dedicated his time to healing the community. *Abuela* and Papi were searching for Frankie while securing the last of the stolen children in homes, near and far. The cartel families and townspeople were consumed by burying and mourning their dead. The various members of the resistance were forming groups and reporting back to Miguel.

Everyone was busy except Maria, who felt as though she was always in the way. Someone had to hide her, stay with her or risk putting her in harms way which was stressful on everyone. Maria asked her mother for permission to begin attending school. Gabriella was initially taken aback by Maria's boldness, but after some consideration she realized that Maria had also been living a "half-life." Maria had asked her mother a million questions about school over the years. Gabriella knew that Maria wanted desperately to be a regular kid one day. She agreed that her daughter could go to school but warned that it would only be temporary. The war was not over, and their future was not secure.

The local school, Escuela Publica de Señor Soto, accepted Maria and agreed to provide her with protection. Maria, excited to make friends her own age, thought that going to school and being a student looked like fun on TV. She was proud to be enrolled in the same school that her mother and Miguel attended; the place where Miguel's own mother had once been a teacher.

The school's expectations and structure were new to Maria. She had never been expected to sit still for so long before. She had never been expected to raise her hand before speaking and being acknowledged by the teacher. Gabriella had been her only tutor, so it was a grueling to adjust at first. But, she liked learning in a classroom in spite of the initial challenges. She came home with stories each day.

The girls were shy to spend time with Maria as they had heard stories that Miguel, the man she often called her Papa, was in charge of the resistance. They didn't want to get too close or they might be punished by the gangs. Maria had been advanced in her studies, earning her respect among her peers and she found she could help some of them when they were puzzled. Helping felt good.

The boys were especially nice to her and tried to teach her to play *fútbol* at lunch break. They had never known anyone who didn't know how to play *fútbol*. They didn't mind being puzzled over schoolwork. She didn't have to mentor them.

Miguel had been dropping Maria off and walking her into class. Later, he'd pick her up. He had spoken to all of Maria's teachers and reminded them that she should never be alone, that they needed to be vigilant at all times. Miguel had made sure that the head teacher kept a pistol with her and knew how to use it.

One day, Miguel asked Gabriella to join him for the ride to school to pick up Maria, but she declined. Workers were fixing the roof of his family home this day, and since Miguel had chosen the workers himself, Gabriella was feeling safe. Besides, she had already begun to cook dinner and didn't want to ruin the meal by rushing.

He teased her, "Oh! That's what is going to ruin our dinner?"

"Hey, I'm new at all this cooking stuff. Give a girl a break already!" Gabriella laughed and encouraged him to go without her.

The three of them had been moving around to sleep in different locations each night for safety reasons, but Miguel loved being able to spend time in his own childhood home. His days were spent meeting with government officials, trying to ensure that they would take the resistance seriously. He was hopeful his daily presence would make it harder for them to be influenced by the cartel. But, he looked forward to his evenings at home.

Miguel arrived early to the schoolhouse, as usual. He scanned the area for unfamiliar cars and unusual people, especially men. He stepped out of the car, checking in the bushes and behind barrels. It was the same routine each day. As he had hoped, everything looked fine. Once back in the car, he let his head settle against the headrest to relax and collect his thoughts.

The local media had not been allowed to air Miguel's speech on TV, but it was posted all over the Internet. American media showed his speech only once, and then they had lost interest. Miguel had received intel that people were responding, though, getting organized with weapons his resistance had distributed.

The media involvement, albeit limited, had been enough to embarrass México's President. Miguel had been assured privately that he had his government's support, which helped Miguel feel slightly safer. Miguel had thought that the government might actually be using the resistance as a way to tip the power scales back in their own favor. Publicly, he still blamed the resistance for the chaos, which meant that the cartel wouldn't exact revenge on the President. Miguel continued to wonder why there had been so much peace since the initial strike.

People in the communities seemed hopeful, though many were crippled with fear as well. Being armed and organized provided strength and gave them faith. A sense of optimism had begun to spring up in the community. Some spoke of Miguel as though he was divine.

News quickly spread of another building filled with child prisoners freed to the South. President Desiderio, claiming full credit for this accomplishment, asserted publicly that he had been working hard against the cartels all along, and that his work was finally paying off. Everyone who watched his broadcast or heard the news recognized his lies. They knew that the resistance was an irritation to him nationally and internationally, and that was the only reason the President did anything resembling good.

President Desiderio Juarez was a proud Mexican, therefore, the one thing he was not going to tolerate was being publicly called out and embarrassed, no matter how true the allegations were. Local media would normally not be allowed to mention cartel-related atrocities, but this time, they broadcasted the story of the freed hostages, and President Juarez spoke of his conquest and dedication to the suppression of the cartels. This change of Presidential-heart had to be good news.

Miguel knew that the cartels at some point would avenge their loss but, they were being patient. It was hard to predict where or when; he just knew that chaos would follow. The most important thing was that for the time being, the resistance had not been disarmed by the government as in previous uprisings. The people involved had always ended up back where they started only worse as there was always a punishment.

Miguel became alert when he heard the sound of students that had begun to flow from the doorway of the school and run to board the buses that would take them home. Some younger students chased each other around and between the trees in a game of tag before they began their walk home. Miguel remembered doing this with Gabriella, always trying to catch her. A smile grew slowly across his face as he recalled being thirteen.

Miguel waited and watched until finally a flood of panic overtook him. Maria hadn't followed the last child from the building. He tried to be patient; maybe she had stopped at the water bubbler, maybe she had dropped a book. A minute seemed like twenty, and he pushed open the car door, unholstered his gun, and ran for the schoolhouse.

He thrust the door open so hard it slammed against the wall, the thud echoed all around him as the door bounced back at him. He leaned on it again as the school became deathly quiet. He quickly turned the corner with his gun held out in front. Maria's classroom came into view. She spotted him and sprang up, standing protectively in front of her friends. The girls screamed.

"Papa!" she shouted, "What is wrong with you?"

Miguel asked, "Are you okay? Why didn't you come out?" Maria collected her things without speaking and ran past Miguel, out into the schoolyard heading for the car. He could hear her whimpering as she flew by.

Once in the car Maria shouted, "Papa, how could you embarrass me like that? That was humiliating! Those girls are just learning to trust me, and now I am sure they will never speak to me again."

"Why didn't you come out?" he asked again.

"Papa, I am helping the girls sometimes when they fall behind. They asked me to stay for a minute to explain something. They say it is easier to learn when I talk about math than it is when the teacher explains. I was proud, Papa. Only the boys would talk to me before, and now you have lost me my only chance with the girls."

"So, the boys talk to you? You have to be careful of the boys, Maria."

"PAPA! I am not going to talk to you about boys, especially right now. This is about you and your over-reacting to every little thing. You make everyone nervous, and no one is going to want to be my friend."

They argued, and Miguel apologized over and over again. He explained that he loved Maria very much, and he only wanted to protect her. He said that they could never be too careful. Maria cried explaining that those first days had been so difficult. She just wanted to feel like a normal a kid and fit in. Miguel was ruining her dream. She complained that she was just starting to feel comfortable. She ran into the house and yelled for Gabriella. Mama would understand and talk to him.

"Mama!" she called out. "Mama, Papa made a fool out of me! Mama?" There was no sound. They were alone in the house. They both called out to Gabriella, but there was no response. The only sounds were that of the workers on the roof. The stove held simmering pots, and nothing appeared disturbed. Gabriella's car was still parked next to the house. Miguel began to feel afraid again.

Miguel called out to the workers on the roof to ask if they had seen anything. They shook their heads to indicate they had not and continued working. With their heads kept facing downward, Miguel could sense that something was wrong. Were they afraid to speak or be punished? "Hey! Where's Gabriella?" Finally one man yelled down that a car had pulled up and left again shortly after, but they hadn't really paid attention. Miguel returned to the house, trying not to panic, but he knew Gabriella had been abducted. He instructed Maria to do her homework, while he dialed Gabriella's cell number. Her phone rang, but it was right there, next to the stove, in the kitchen. He dialed the police.

***

Frankie had apologized to Gabriella on the phone and had said that he wanted to see her. He said he needed to talk to her.

"Frankie! I am so happy to hear your voice. Where have you been? We have been looking for you. Your wife is as worried as we are. We are going to eat at Miguel's house. I'm cooking! Can you come?"

He said he was on his way and hung up abruptly. She had been worried about him since he disappeared from the marketplace ten days before. Hearing a car pull up in front of the house, Gabriella looked out to see Frankie's familiar face waiting there. She ran to the end of the driveway, where he had asked her to take a ride with him.

Craning her neck to look inside the car, she said, "Frankie, you look horrible. Are you okay? Where have you been?"

Frankie didn't answer but hit the unlock button for her to get in. Gabriella glanced back toward the house and saw the two men watching her from the roof. They didn't appear concerned though they should have, as Miguel had hand-picked the men who would work on his house to also provide protection. The men looked away and began to work again. She stepped into the car and closed the door, deciding to speak with the two workers right after talking to Frankie.

They drove in silence for a couple minutes until Gabriella softly asked, "Frankie, where have you been? We looked for you, but no one knew anything. I worried that you were dead." He turned his face away from her. She touched his shoulder, and he flinched. Frankie was speeding and clearly agitated. "Frankie, talk to me. Whatever it is, we will fix it. We have been through so much together, and I'm sure that we can fix this too. Just talk to me." She could see he was becoming increasingly more upset. Sweat dripped from his forehead. Something was very wrong. Her heart began to pound so hard that she could hear it in her ears. He was stifling a sob when he began to explain.

"Gabriella, you are not safe. Santino's gangs have someone new in charge. Miguel is not in danger for now, but they want you. They know you killed Santino. Do you understand what this means?"

"It's bad, Frankie, but we have always known this might happen. I will be extra careful."

"NO, Gabriella!" he shouted. "It's not like that. You think you had it hard, locked up in that house, but you didn't. You don't understand. They are going to get you, and they will torture you. You have really no idea." She was starting to believe him.

Gabriella had never seen Frankie get upset. His face was contorting with tears running down his cheeks.

Frankie explained that he had no choice. The new leader was demanding that Gabriella and Miguel pay for what they had done. They had put a price on Gabriella's head for her capture. "They are planning to torture you and eventually kill you. They want to first make Miguel live without you, to make him crazy with grief, knowing that you are being tortured. They will pay 500,000 pesos for you." Gabriella stared at Frankie, slowly grasping the seriousness of the situation.

"What do you mean you have no choice?"

"Gabriella, I've been ordered. Santino's replacement wants me to bring you to him."

"You're not going to do that Frankie, right? You wouldn't do that to me, would you?" Panic was taking over her mind.

"I could never do that to you. I do have to protect you though. Gabriella, they are going to kill me no matter what. If don't bring you back, they will find you, but I will already be dead. I won't be able to protect you. I have to kill you before they can hurt you. I have to make sure that you don't suffer."

Gabriella sat in stunned silence. Frankie extracted a nearly drained liter of Walesa vodka from beside his seat and gulped down several long, hard swallows. She pleaded, "Frankie, you don't have to kill me. Give me an opportunity to try to protect myself. I'd have a chance. We have already accomplished so much. This is not the time to give up."

Frankie pulled the car off the road and stopped. Dust encircled the car. "Get out."

Gabriella didn't move, but Frankie stepped out and with difficulty, slowly limped around the car, opening her door. She could see that he was in obvious pain. Gabriella had never been so frightened and had no thoughts of what to do. Her life was unraveling in front of her. This didn't seem real; it was not happening to her. She was unable to comprehend what she was hearing.

"The men working on your roof were going bring you to Maximo, Santino's replacement. I was almost too late. Gabriella, they will pull out your fingernails; one at a time. They will tie you up, and each will rape you every day, but they will do it with things that will tear at you. They will boil your feet in water, they will cut off your hands, they will beat you." He cried, "There is a basement in Santino's house and most of it is filled with instruments for torture. Starvation is the least of the cruel things they will do to you."

His face reddened. As Frankie hobbled backing away from the car, Gabriella could see that he was badly hurt. She asked, "Why are you limping? What did they do to you?"

Frankie began to rip open his shirt, showing her a blackened abdomen. Large ugly stitches ran the length of his torso from his ribs to his belt. Gabriella attempted to hide the pain and fear she felt behind her hands as she pressed them over her mouth. Someone had cut out his kidney. "That's not all, Gabriella." He cried and looked down toward his groin. "They took it all. They said I was a coward for helping you and a man shouldn't have balls if he won't use them. Gabriella, they didn't anesthetize me. They are going to do this to you too!" Frankie had begun sobbing so hard his eyes squeezed shut and his mouth hung open with grief. He raised his gun to sight a shot.

Gabriella stepped out of the car and begged Frankie to reconsider. "Please! We can fight them. Maria needs me. Please, Frankie, you are like a father to me. I always knew you were watching over me. Frankie, I beg you. There has to be another way."

Frankie's hands trembled as he cried openly. He couldn't stop talking, continually apologizing. "I'm sorry, Gabriella. I love you. You don't understand what they will do to you. I am not crazy. I am protecting you. This is the only way."

Frankie had the gun pointed at her, struggling to steady his hands. Gabriella was petrified; convinced that Frankie was right, that the cartel would find her and do these terrible things to her.

She was terrified of being tortured. But, she was also wary from being brave; tired of the killing and of remembering those mutilated children over and over in her dreams.

Tears poured down her cheeks. Gabriella's legs faltered and she fell to her knees, too disoriented to stand, she closed her eyes. The sound of a shot caused her flinch, but silence followed. Two more shots rang out. Frankie's hands had shaken violently, and he was so weak from his wounds that he wasn't able to hold the gun steady through the kickback as he fired. Confused, Gabriella opened her eyes to see Frankie falling to kneel on all fours on the ground, his strength waning.

"Please Frankie. Calm down. It's going to be all right. See, we are not supposed to die today. That's why you missed." Gabriella couldn't bear to see her friend so ruined. He had always been a gentleman through all the years that she that she had been held captive by Santino.

"I'm sorry." He was looking at her as he turned the gun toward his own chin and shot. His lower jaw hung grotesquely off the side of his face. Thick, red blood was splashed all around.

Gabriella cried out, "Frankie! No." It was all happing so fast. She stood up and walked toward Frankie on trembling legs. "You're a good man, Frankie. I love you like I loved my own father." Frankie pointed the gun at his temple this time. "Please. I am begging you. I need you." Frankie made gurgling sounds as he tried to speak; his eyes darting around. Guilt pressed in on Gabriella. She was the reason that Frankie had been tortured. The humiliation of being so disfigured would be unbearable for him. Her heart ached for him, but she knew she had to get him go, "I will tell stories of your greatness until I can no longer speak. I will not let the cartel get me. I will get them. You will be remembered as a hero. A legend. Thank you for warning me. Thank you for everything." He closed his eyes and fired.

***

Two officers had arrived at the house and Miguel had begun frantically begging them for help. Each officer calmly stuck a hand out to be shaken by Miguel. Puzzled, he shook each. One officer suggested they talk in the house. Frankie's SUV came screaming into view as the men turned to enter. They all froze until Miguel yelled, "That's Gabriella!"

She opened the door and revealed blood covered clothes and hands. She looked up to the roof where the workers were still occupied, and waited for them to look down at her. When they didn't, she yelled, "Go get them! I need to talk to them!" The policemen drew their guns and called for the men come down. Putting their hands in the air, the workers dropped to the ground without further instructions. The police cuffed them, ordering them to walk toward the house.

Once inside, Gabriella flew at the two workers. Her hand clung to the shirt of one and she asked through gritted teeth, "How did they get to you? How would you have killed me?" She looked carefully at their frightened faces; these two men were people she trusted.

Without hesitation, Gabriella delivered a knee to the first worker's groin; he collapsed onto the floor. The second took a blow to the head from the butt end of her pistol and dropped next to the first. She aimed her gun from one to the next, "Start talking."

The first worker muttered, "There is a bounty on your head of 500,000 pesos. Cartelistas came and told us to capture you; here, today. They don't really ask though," he explained. "We would have been punished if we didn't follow their orders."

"Someone is going to get that money," the second grunted. "We need that money, it may as well be us. They would have killed you anyway."

Gabriella fired her gun twice and watched them die.

Neither officer moved, their jaws slack with surprise. Miguel screamed, "Gabriella, that's wrong! You can't just kill people. Those men may have families!"

She screamed back, her face almost unrecognizable, "If I let had them go free, others would have come tomorrow. I'm sending a message to the new leader of the cartel. These men would have been tortured and killed anyway when they went back without me. If you don't believe me, go down the street and see what they did to Frankie. It was merciful of me to kill them! If they did have children, their children are better off without cowardly fathers. The gang leaders need to understand that we will continue to fight as hard as they will."

Gabriella was struggling to regain her composure. She couldn't fill her lungs with air, "This is not what I want," she mumbled before a fit anxiety and rage took over again. She looked like she was on the verge of losing her mind. She groaned and sobbed.

Pointing to the street, she finally managed to say, "Frankie… down the road. Those monsters have been torturing him since he disappeared from the marketplace. He was going to kill me to save me from the same fate. They cut him up, Miguel. They cut him up." The gun dropped from her hand and she fell, slumping into a chair. Miguel was without words. He was sure Gabriella would be arrested. He didn't know what to do.

The two officers took control of the situation. "She's right, Miguel. You are all in a bad spot, and it's going to get worse. That's a tremendous amount of money to offer people in this poor community. Look, you have more friends than you know and we want our freedom back, too. We remember happier times, and we want you to win this. We will do what we can to help you. Remember though, we are no good to you dead, so there are limits."

The two officers agreed to take the two dead workers with them and collect Frankie's body on their way. The police report would show that the three had been found together, already dead. Miguel opened his wallet and offered cash, but the officers refused saying, "We are indebted to you already. You have given us hope that life can get better. Safer. You rescued all those young children. We can't thank you enough." Each officer shook Miguel's hand again before leaving.

11

Pedro

Miguel sat on the floor outside the bedroom door and listened to the shower water turn off. He could hear Gabriella move about the room, opening drawers and closing them. Finally, he heard her land on the bed; it squeaked under her weight. The faint sound of sobbing broke free from the room. He turned, leaning his body against the door. He wanted to go to Gabriella, to comfort her but he wasn't sure what to say or do. He was accustomed to her beautiful face, so familiar, but he did not know or understand the person behind the door.

Maria had been crying on the sofa in the living room since she had arrived home from school. She had witnessed many horrible situations at the club, but never anything like this. The stress of seeing her mother this upset was overwhelming, she flinched at the slightest sound. Watching her own mother execute two men without hesitation had been devastating. It was clear to Miguel that Gabriella would need to go into hiding, but he wasn't sure whether that would be enough to keep her safe. How to help Maria weighed heavily on his mind as well. School had been a very therapeutic and Maria had seemed happy once she had begun to adjust. But, Miguel had to face the fact that Maria would no longer be safe. Perhaps she may never have been secure even with all of the precautions that had been taken by those around her.

Maria stood from the curled position in which she had been resting in on the couch, and headed for the bedroom door. She touched Miguel's hair as she passed him, twisting the door knob to enter and join her mother on the bed. At least they would comfort each other, he thought. He stayed at the door and listened to the muffled sounds filtering out of the room. Gabriella had begun to hum a lullaby to Maria. All would be well for now.

The rumble of an engine on the street outside the house caught Miguel's attention and he pulled himself up to see where the sound was coming from. An eighteen-wheeler ambled down the street. This was the first time a truck this size had ever been in this rural neighborhood. Miguel was curious, but self-defense being his top priority, he checked for his weapon.

With an ear-to-ear grin, Pedro materialized, as if out of thin air. He blasted the horn, backing the truck up beside Miguel's house. The cab door opened and Pedro leapt to the ground announcing, "Special delivery!"

Pedro's energy enabled Miguel to momentarily forget the sadness inside the house, and he let go a hardy laugh. He stretched his arms out and warmly embraced his friend.

"You, *mi amigo*, are a sight for sore eyes. Welcome. What's in the truck?"

"Gifts from the American military and their poorly managed inventory system," he said mockingly.

The two men spent a long time sitting together and talking. At first, Miguel related all the horrors and successes of the last couple weeks. It had been less than a month since they last met, but it felt like a lifetime. So much had happened.

"We suffered a great loss today, and Gabriella is taking it harder than all of us. We all desperately need something or someone to renew our confidence, and now you are here! *Gracias a dios*. Thanks to God."

Eventually, Gabriella and Maria emerged from the house to join the two men. Pedro wrapped himself around Gabriella, lifting her off of her feet. Miguel noticed the tone of the conversation change. They were soon chatting like the children they were when the three were last together. They tried to recall the names of different kids from school, reminiscing about how relentlessly the three friends had playfully provoked each other. They tried to recall how many detentions they each had received, Gabriella boasting she had none, and the associated misdeeds for which they were given. They laughed and hugged. Pedro's company was a both gift and a great relief.

***

While Miguel had to keep himself out of sight, Pedro was free to go wherever he wanted. If anyone recognized him, no one would question why he had returned; he had completed a Middle East tour for the US government and was visiting his hometown of Esperanza.

Pedro possessed liberal amounts of nervous energy, an irritating trait during periods of rest, however, a treasured endowment during war-time. He decided that they needed to keep a closer eye on things and put his military training, technical surveillance, to work. Things were overall too quiet. He took over an empty office space on the third floor of a corner building in the marketplace. From this vantage point, he would be able to watch the marketplace area as well as the roads in and out. Pedro would stock-pile weapons there and fortify the door with explosives in case they were discovered.

He installed cameras and recording equipment and hooked it all up to his laptop. He slipped a tracking devise on any vehicle suspected of trouble. He wanted to know where to locate them should he need to. He had mastered the art of war and was happiest when his mind was occupied.

Miguel wondered if Gabriella felt safest when she was with Pedro. She still spent time with their men to keep moral up, and share any news, but mostly, Gabriella spent time with Pedro. There was so much he could teach her that she really wanted to know. She liked watching the dots blinking on his computer screen and then mapping out where the gangs spent their time. Sometimes they would drive by these locations just to see for themselves what was of interest there. Miguel accused Pedro of showing off for Gabriella. Pedro retorted that Miguel was jealous.

Gabriella found Pedro easy to talk to, as he shared in the anger that she carried within her. He praised her for being bold, especially with her weapon. He taught her how to think of killing as her responsibility. "This was war," he would say. He stressed that her lack of fear would be a key to winning back their home permanently. The others had begun to look up to her. Stories of her bravery were spreading and giving everyone courage. No one knew exactly how she had managed to killed Santino, but they knew she fought him bravely and took his life. As far as people were concerned, she had killed the devil himself and they were thankful. She was becoming somewhat of a local legend.

Pedro made it clear that he was as excited by her fearlessness as everyone else. "You are beautiful, strong and very sexy, Gabby. This 'legend thing' is just hot." This made her laugh, which was such a relief. Gabriella liked feeling powerful and respected. She liked being hot. Spending time with Pedro made her feel confident and found she missed him when they weren't working together. Everything seemed so clear and safe when he was nearby.

Since Pedro had arrived home, he had stopped getting high. Gabriella could see the hint of curls that bent where they began filling in all over his head. His face had lost its sunken look as he began to gain some weight. He shaved only occasionally keeping a rugged stubble on his checks. That big toothy grin of his just seemed to grow wider. Pedro looked genuinely happy to be back in Esperanza, but happy to be "at war" as well.

Gabriella had not recovered from her ordeal with Frankie. Her body ached just thinking about what the cartelistas had done to him and she spoke to him in prayer as though it might comfort him. She imagined that Frankie was still alive, watching over her, and was surprised at times to look around the room and not see him standing there. She told Pedro that she needed to think about him; to remember his sacrifice. She claimed that she deliberately let the anger boil inside her so that she could be ready to fight. She refused to let Frankie go.

Gabriella burned to find a way into the torture chamber where Frankie's life had been ruined. She wanted to blow it up. Somehow, she felt that if she could erase the place, she might erase his pain. The risk was too great, and she knew it. If she wasn't careful, she might end up there anyway. She focused her energy on communication and strategizing with the men.

With Pedro controlling surveillance, Miguel had continued focusing on the government side of things. While he spent every afternoon with Maria, his mornings were dedicated to making arrangements and talking with local police and the mayor himself. He was unsettled by the calmness that had set in. He still allowed Maria to attend school but kept the attendance to an erratic pattern that might help to discourage an attack.

The poor mayor was on the verge of insanity. It was clear that he was receiving constant pressure from both sides and had turned to drugs for comfort. Mayor Ernesto was losing weight and hair; his cheeks began to hollow and his clothes weren't fitting well. The elaborate decor of his office only exaggerated his poor physical and mental condition.

México's President Desiderio had seized the opportunity to regain control of his ailing country with the ever growing band of rebels, so Mayor Ernesto was expected to cooperate with Miguel.

But the local pressure to overlook criminal behavior kept the mayor second-guessing himself, plucking on his last nerve.

Miguel could see for himself that there was a consistent police presence in public places. Patrols had been added at bus stops, schools, factories and all the locations from which people had previously been abducted. The same was happening all over México. Drugs were being manufactured and moved without interference from the government, and the cartels were getting by without collecting their extra taxes. But there were reports of many altercations between gangs and police.

The police continued to avoid the gangs, and the gangs were not interested in behaving. Both sides attempted to assert their authority, and both sides suffered losses as a result. The overcrowded Mexican prisons were beginning to bust at the seams, but the graveyard's steady stream of new arrivals caused the most anxiety. The resistance suffered losses as well as the police and gangs too.

Miguel was also told stories of trouble involving the merchants. Gang members entered businesses, attempting to collect taxes and shots were fired. No one reemerged, not on their own two feet anyway. The dead cartelista's vehicles were finding their way to Sharkie's place, where he made them untraceable and either sold them or gave them to the resistance.

And, the resistance was growing. It was growing so large that it was becoming hard to control and organize. Some of the men put themselves in charge of large groups, which were forming smaller groups of men who either liked each other or were extremely effective working together. Other groups formed based on logistics, like the proximity of their homes. Some men couldn't get along.

In many ways, time and size were taking a toll on the resistance. Closer contact and strong leadership was necessary, but communication was difficult. Miguel sent messages via cell phone and often used the Internet, but it wasn't always reliable. His efforts weren't enough or secure.

Some men grumbled they were still waiting to be issued an SUV; others complained that they needed money. Many said they needed to get back to work, while others just felt unrecognized and unimportant, receiving insufficient accolades for their hard work. A few men had become too comfortable with their new authority, testing the limits of their power by demanding free lunch or free gas when in town. They saw it as payment for standing up to the cartel.

***

Since the coup, guests of the mayor had not been not allowed weaponry and were patted down at the door prior to visiting with him in the office. Late one afternoon, four men entered the mayor's office, refused to be frisked and headed directly toward his office door. Before they could reach the door, the resistance, who kept constant vigil at the office, blinded them with pepper spray and disarmed them. The men continued to fight until finally their hands were bound and they were under control.

These men were clearly dangerous. The resistance needed to discover what these men had wanted with the Mayor and why they were armed, but the men refused to talk. When the detainees wouldn't cooperate, a phone call was made and instructions were given, "Bring them to the Gates of Hell and hold them there. They'll talk."

Once the evening sky became black, the resistance led the four men out the back door of the office where a car was waiting. They were driven to "the Gates of Hell," the cement building where the abducted children had been held captive only a few weeks before.

The group used night vision goggles and travelled slowly down the roads with their headlights turned off. They couldn't risk being spotted, though no one had been seen in or near the building since the last of the victims' remains had been taken away. The land mines had been removed, but the holes remained like pockmarks on what was once a flawless face. The pitted, disfigured terrain made retracing their steps effortless yet eerie.

Gabriella and Pedro met up with the group there. Gabriella could feel herself wilting as they approached the building. The sickening odor of death and decay still hung in the crisp, night air. Gabriella usually felt brave and adventurous with Pedro, but not this time. Now she felt sick. He, on the other hand, seemed exhilarated.

Once inside the windowless, cement building, Gabriella's spine shuddered in disgust, but she tried to act like she was in charge and comfortable with whatever would happen next.

She had ordered that the four-foot containers be reorganized so that they could hold grown men. The bloody table and all the filthy surgical instruments had been left. Nothing had been cleaned after the corpses had been removed, so the foul stink of rot loomed in the air as thick as a bank of fog on an English moor.

The four cartelistas were young and fit; they had rebellion in their eyes. Gabriella had never interrogated anyone before and wasn't sure how to begin. The captives seemed to think that they had the emotional advantage, but watching the boxes being constructed clearly had them concerned. Gabriella began by asking what the men were doing at the mayor's office, to which there was no reply. She asked calmly who had sent them there. Her question remained unanswered. She instructed her men to cage two of the cartelistas. She could see that this situation was shaking their resolve as they fought to break away.

The two men struggled at the mouth of the enclosure as though they might lose their minds if the door was locked. As the wire from the bottom of the cages had been replaced with a solid floor, once the door was secured the only air available was through the six inch long slit in the side of the container, originally designed for the passage of food. There wasn't enough space inside for the men to move and immediately it became too hot. Their faces couldn't reach the air hole, and they became quiet.

The other two wore angry expressions, acting insulted rather than frightened. Gabriella hadn't been prepared for this. She had seen everything going differently in her mind and she was terrified to think of what she might have to do to force these men to cooperate.

Gabriella ordered her men to cuff the two remaining cartelistas to the floor by one leg and kept their hands tied. Stepping around them, she finally rested herself against the bloody table where the brown crusted tools waited. She hoped that the men were thinking that she was familiar with the reason that the table was bloody, that she might use these tools on them. Gabriella saw their expressions waver slightly, but they were still no in the mood to relent.

She asked them about Frankie. She asked them who had cut him. She could tell by their faces that they had either been involved with Frankie's torture or were at least aware of it. They seemed suddenly uncomfortable.

Pedro watched Gabriella but didn't utter a word. His eyes sparked with excitement, and she realized that this was not the first time he had been involved in extracting information from prisoners. She slowly picked up a knife from the table, wanting to appear impressive, and twisted it around in her hand. Her stomach lurching, she hoped that her expression would not betray her. Gabriella's mind kept seeing the blood and the poor children she had rescued. She returned the knife to the table, hoping that her relief was not obvious. She was not capable of finishing what she had begun.

"I don't know what to do with you. I don't want to kill all four of you, but I may have to. You have proven yourselves a threat. I need to know who you work for, if you are from Santino's cartel or another. We were hoping that we could achieve peace. These attacks cannot be allowed; you cannot assassinate government officials and get away with it. I really wish you would cooperate, but maybe you need time to think about it." Gabriella glanced at Pedro and headed for the door with Pedro following her. She was shaking and upset so he reached his arms around her and whispered that he would take care of everything from this point on. He lifted Gabriella's chin with his finger and kissed her mouth. She tried to resist the tingle of excitement that washed over her when Pedro's lips touched hers, but she needed this too much. Kissed him back, her hands grasped at him instinctively. Pedro pulled himself away and watched Gabriella try to compose herself. He flashed a triumphant smile, while Gabriella's expression became angry. Without a word, she opened the door and stepped into the car. She looked back at the building and then at Pedro.

"I may be a while. I'll see you later?" he asked.

"No. Please don't. Not tonight. I need to think." She drove away alone.

12

Maximo

Six SUV's rolled up into the marketplace. Four gunmen emerged from each and chose a post from which to guard. The townspeople were always nervous when the SUV's arrived, and Miguel remembered back to the day that he pulled Gabriella into the alley after hearing them in the distance. Anger boiled up inside him. The events of that day had been terrifying, and the lifelong consequences still reverberated, haunting every moment since.

With the guards scanning the area for signs of trouble, someone helped Maximo, the newly appointed head of the cartel, out of the car and onto his feet. His feet shuffled along the street quietly and slowly. He stared toward the gathering townspeople as though searching for a welcoming face among them, but there were none. He was not a large man, nor was he a strong one. He was long past youth, his clothes were not tailored and he was not clean-shaven. He looked like the average citizen of Esperanza.

Maximo reached into his pocket and removed a stack of pesos. People became still and watched him in silence. He extended his arm toward a woman standing close by and stepped forward offering her 100 pesos. Without speaking, she carefully reached out, accepting the money with a polite nod. Maximo did this again and again.

He smiled, patting the heads of some of the young ones, seeming pleased to have an audience. The gentle touches, the upturned corners of his mouth, and his unexpected generosity all suggested to Miguel that Maximo wanted to be comfortable among the people. He very likely celebrated grand festivals on these same streets when he was young. He must have experienced the warmth of friendship and laughter here. Miguel thought it looked like Maximo craved that fondness now.

The resistance had filtered in amongst the people. Some were given pesos by Maximo himself. The military was also spread strategically around the plaza.

Miguel waited unaccompanied at a table on the periphery of the square, watching these events unfold. Miguel was more frightened to meet with this man today than he had been during his speech in the open air at the same marketplace just three weeks before. He had felt sure that he was not going to make it through his speech that day before someone shot him, and he had the same feeling of doom today.

Maximo finally joined Miguel at his table, ordering drinks and a snack of bread and dipping oil. "Thank you for meeting me on this beautiful day." Maximo said. *"Gracias a Dios* for this beautiful day." They struggled to make small talk, but after several long silences Maximo began, "That was an impressive speech you made. The people were very moved. I was moved." Miguel nodded thanks. "How do you actually see this playing out, Miguel?"

"I see you scaling back until the people are safe." Miguel said. "It's just that simple. The contraband is not my immediate concern."

"Miguel, I can't just step aside and let you invite people to Disney Land. It's not all happy endings, you know? You've already cost me a substantial amount of money."

"You've cost me a great deal too." Miguel said. "When I was a boy, I lived in this town. Did you know that? I played here and learned here and loved here. This was my home. Until the day that the cartel invaded. A woman was beheaded there." He pointed to a spot in the street not far from them. "An innocent woman. She was a mother, and cartelistas cut her head off."

"I am sorry for that. That is not the way I want things to be."

"Can you promise that your gangs will never do anything like that again?"

"No. I cannot. I do not control the men. They do these things of free will."

"They do them with your consent."

"Do not mistake my intention. I sell drugs. That is what my organization does. Americans demand narcotics; I supply them. And I protect those in my organization."

"You do worse than sell drugs. You harvest organs and sell sex slaves. You raid towns and behead innocent people. You impose taxes on businesses that cannot thrive under the burden of the extra expense. And, you abduct those who don't pay."

Maximo stopped eating and sat back in his chair. He spun the stem of his wine glass between his fingers before lifting it to his lips. He spent a long time thinking before he responded. Miguel was surprised to learn what a patient man Maximo was.

"Organs are harvested and prostitutes are sold for one reason only. The United States demands these things. If my men do not provide them, someone else will. I don't encourage it. I just take a cut of the profits, the price of doing business in my district. The means by which all of this is accomplished is not my concern. My concern is that the narcotics business grows, and my organization gets a cut of whatever other industry operates within my territory."

Maximo spoke as he ate, pacing himself, being careful to have finished each bite before speaking again. Miguel's stomach knotted up, and he couldn't push food into it, so he watched Maximo and listened. He was surprised at how civilized and calm Maximo was.

"Even with your cousin Santino's strong leadership, the other cartels cut into my business interests. The government needs their slice of respect, and now I have you to deal with. It's not easy. We are successful because of fear. Fear suppresses the people so that I can run my business.

Miguel, we have both suffered many losses since you began this quest, but you have no chance of getting what you want. You have to let it go. I can make sure that you are not harmed if you stop now. You are still Santino's cousin after all, and you are caring for his daughter."

"The difference between our losses is great," Miguel said. "Each innocent person who you have murdered matters. They matter to me, to their families, to the world. Each of your losses are mere inconveniences. There is always a hungry desperado waiting for his chance to achieve power or wealth. The life lost on your side is not even mourned before he is replaced."

Maximo's face hardened, and again, he waited before speaking. "Miguel, that is a harsh thing to say. My people are my family; I owe them protection, and I will always protect them. You can count on that. I don't, however, control them. I don't think you understand that even I do not choose the terms of my business. The industry I have chosen is driven by nothing more than the dark side of human nature. It is a nasty business. But, what you are attempting to fight is human nature. A force that has not evolved over time.

Think about history, Miguel. All of human thought and actions stem from a need to survive that is pre-programmed into our primal brains, much like an infant who suckles at its mothers breast within seconds of drawing its first breath. Human beings have no choice in this matter. We will always find a way to survive. What eventually does evolve in a man's brain is the way he feels about his method of survival. We become desensitized. We change our definition of what is right or wrong based on the results of our actions.

If a starving man is rewarded with food, he will learn to enjoy the reward and overlook the means by which he has acquired the sustenance. If a man, unable to provide for his family discovers a way to provide for them, he soon learns to overlook that method and bask in the warmth of the pride that comes with having a home, groceries, and power."

"I spelled out the terms in my speech." Miguel said. "The local businesses will pay the government taxes only; you will continue to grow, make and sell your drugs. You will always be a wealthy man. How much money does a man who hides out in caves and slums need to be happy? To have peace?"

"When the other cartels have more wealth than I, they will possess the means to buy more politicians and employees, more.... "desperados," as you call them. Then, you and I will both be out of business. I will not be powerful enough to fight them off and neither will you. Then what?" Maximo countered.

"Do you understand that people have learned to live with the drug culture?" Miguel asked. "No one will challenge that. America needs her drugs. It's the violence that we can no longer tolerate.

Wouldn't you be proud to live in a community that thrives? You could take the credit. Can you see yourself walking down the streets and having people love you because you made their lives better? You are a powerful man, a man the townspeople can teach their children to look up to because you provide security, schools, churches. With your money, you could become a legend. Like the Virgin of Guadalupe, they will pray to you when you are gone, and you will never be forgotten. You will live forever in their memory as a... a person they loved."

"You are a good man, Miguel. You have honorable intentions, but you are naive. If you think that I control the behavior of the gangs, you would be wrong. These men, they are hungry, ambitious. They work for me to distribute the drugs, but create their own business opportunities after that. I require a cut of what they earn, but I do not encourage them to do the things that they do.

As I said before, you are trying to fight human nature, and you will lose. It has taken the human race millions and millions of years to evolve to who we are today. But, we have only lived in communities for six thousand years. In comparison, that is not much time. Our primal brains have not evolved, we are not equipped, with the intellect to peacefully live together. In desperate times, we still think like prehistoric individuals. By the time our brains evolve so that we can live together peacefully, humanity will have destroyed itself. There's a bit of irony." Maximo waved his fork like a finger as he spoke.

Miguel's mind raced to work through the theory that Maximo presented. He found his mouth gapping, jaw slack, as he attempted to form a response. "I can't.... I concede that... you may have a point. A sophisticated—incredulous—point. But, evolution and corruption are not related. The cartel is encouraging corruption and that is what has ruined México."

"Corruption, Miguel, is not a thing by itself. It is the result of something else. Simply stated, corruption is the unavoidable consequence of people who make decisions that benefit themselves, like before communities existed, without regard for the whole unit. Look around. Can you think of a country anywhere on the globe that is not plagued by corruption? One does not exist. People in power cannot resist the temptation to take advantage of others. One selfish unethical decision at a time, people in power, and people desperate for power, construct corrupt societies. A corrupt government is nothing more than the inevitable conclusion of collecting and empowering people who would have had to have achieved divinity to escape the unavoidable want for personal gain. I choose to be powerful. What do you choose?"

Miguel's mind groped to find words as impressive as Maximo's. He was not prepared to explain his values persuasively. "I choose... not to hurt other people. Life at the top sounds secure the way you describe it, but it demands that I blacken my soul.

Perhaps, Maximo, some people have evolved. I know that corporate greed and government corruption lead to a morally bankrupt society. This is what you have created. People will follow an honorable leader."

"Is that who you are? A prophet. You fancy yourself an honorable leader, above the fray? You will do better than all of those who came before you? We'll see about that. Time will be the test."

"That is not what I am saying. I am not trying to be a prophet." Miguel had lost the verbal battle. He could hear the tension in his own voice as his pitch grew higher.

"Look, Miguel, when America does not have kidneys and livers to implant, there will be hell to pay. America wants what she wants. The network is large and those at the top don't think about those at the bottom. I could not stop prostitution if I spent the rest of my life trying. It has existed since the beginning of time. I merely take a bit of the profit when the industry is within my borders. As long as there is a demand, there will be a supply."

Maximo glanced at his watch and then signaled the waiter for the bill. He sipped his wine and posed a question to Miguel, "Do you control all of your rebels? Do they all adhere to your principles or do they make their own judgments? Perhaps they apply their own values in the same way that my men think for themselves." Miguel wondered if he was referring to Gabriella playing target practice with his men after Frankie died, or if there were other extreme acts of resistance violence. He wondered if there was another problem, something else that he wasn't aware of.

"I will think about you, Miguel... about our conversation. I will consider your ambitions, but I will not tolerate much more. I have been patient with you. You have cost me many people and considerable income. We will meet again another day very soon." Maximo stood as if to leave.

"How can I reach you? Can I call you? Do you have a phone number?" Miguel asked anxiously.

"Use this number" Maximo scrawled a phone number onto a napkin. "Tell the person who answers it what your concern is. He will take the message for you."

"Do you want my phone number?"

Maximo laughed. "I don't need your phone number to reach you, Miguel. I can reach you anywhere, any time. But, I already have it. I arranged this meeting, don't forget."

13

Bad News

Gabriella flipped her keys in her hand as she walked to meet Miguel, who was busily putting up a hammock in the yard. He spent as much time working in the yard as he could when he was at home. It made him feel proud to have the property look cared for. He imagined that his mother was watching over him and that she was pleased. Gabriella noticed that his efforts were really beginning to pay off; it looked like a home again, like the people who lived there lived well.

"What have you been up to?" Miguel asked.

"Same as always," Gabriella shrugged. "I've been breaking my own neck looking over my shoulders and trying to stay out of sight. We've got some guns ready for shipment to the South, which completes the distribution to all five major cartels. Your father is going to fly them this time. We have been trying to find a safe place to land.

Padre Cayo still needs help. He's happy to see the pews so crowded that people have to stand during Mass, but those who are not looking for medicine are there so Padre can find them a safe place to live. They want him to send them North to safety. Most believe that the cartels will exert their power again. They think the attacks will be worse than ever, and they are afraid.

They want Padre to get them into America, he says he can't do it. The border has changed. It's much more dangerous for illegals right now. How did your meeting with Maximo go?"

"I don't think he is going to kill me," Miguel said. "At least not right now. That's something, I guess. I tried to convince him that investing in real businesses would be more profitable than he thinks, and that it would really help the people. He kept smiling and shaking his head. He called me naive."

"You are naive. And idealistic." Gabriella laughed. "Both of those qualities are good. I don't mean it as in insult."

Miguel continued, "Maximo has a theory. He believes that we humans are not capable of permanently doing good because our brains have not had the time to fully evolve yet. We still can't think beyond survival and the protection of our families, like it was six thousand years ago before civilizations. He thinks that every person who ascends to power has to watch the masses destroy themselves because people are too feeble to understand what it takes to make a community thrive. I have to admit, I actually thought that he may be right. It made sense when he was saying it."

Miguel finished making the last adjustment to the hammock, flopping himself into it. It was an ungraceful landing but once he adjusted himself, he sighed and invited Gabriella to join him by patting the spot next to himself. She smiled, saying that she hoped her landing might be a bit steadier and plopped herself next to him. The hammock swung back and forth a bit, and Gabriella found herself forced to cuddle with Miguel. Miguel folded his arms behind his head and she settled in, resting against the bare skin of his arm. This was the closest to him she had allowed herself to be and it felt awkward at first. He placed one foot on the ground and continued to rock them.

"Did your mother have a song she sang to you when you were young?" Miguel asked.

Gabriella nodded and then began to sing it to Miguel in a quiet, silky voice. She watched him as she sang, while he focused the sky and clouds. A tear formed in the corner of his eye and Gabriella wiped it away. She touched his nose with her finger, and Miguel smiled. She ran her finger over his lips and he kissed it before it slipped onto his chin. Gabriella traced his neck, settling her hand lightly on Miguel's chest. She had to fight the urge to slip her hand into Miguel's shirt to feel his skin. Gabriella let her finger draw circles around one of Miguel's buttons as she finished her song.

"Maria used to hum that song when she stayed with me in Arizona. It's a beautiful song." Miguel confessed that he couldn't remember his own mother's song, admitting that his heart ached at the loss. He worried that his memories of his mother were fading away. It felt like he had forgotten her by forgetting her song.

Miguel's thoughts drifted back to those from his meeting, "Maximo said something else that has been bothering me. He asked me if I am able to control all of the members of our resistance. It made me question whether people may be breaking away from our goal and doing their own thing. What do you think, Gabriella? Should I try to bring everyone together and talk to them?"

She paused while shame forced Gabriella's face to flush. Heavy with guilt she said, "I don't think the whole group should ever be together. There are too many now anyway. There is no way to even fit everyone under one roof." She continued in a calmer tone, "Things are going well, Miguel. There have been some problems, for sure. There have been disagreements between the men, but I don't think you have anything to worry about."

Pedro arrived and joined Miguel and Gabriella in the shade. It was unusual for the three of them to be together. Miguel asked, "Where have you been, Pedro? You stink like death." Pedro looked at Gabriella and then back to Miguel, who seemed momentarily perplexed. Climbing out of the hammock, he began to pace clearly ill at ease. Gabriella sat up, waiting. "Pedro, where have you been?" Miguel repeated.

"Do you need to know everywhere that I go? It seems a bit controlling, *mi amigo*. How was your meeting?" Pedro attempted to change the subject.

"I can think of only one place that can cause a man to smell as bad as you do. I just can't fathom a reason why you would be there." Pedro turned to walk away, but Gabriella called him back saying, "Miguel, four men went to the mayor's office last week to kill him. They were going to do it with their bare hands if they could and leave him sitting in his office chair. Our people restrained them, calling Pedro for instructions. We didn't know what to do with them so we decided to take them to the "Gates of Hell." We've been holding them there. We've been trying to extract information from them."

Miguel shoved Pedro in the chest, throwing a punch that missed its mark. Gabriella screamed, "It's not his fault! It's mine! I did it. I was my idea."

Miguel turned and yelled into Gabriella face, "You are out of control. I don't know the person you have become. You lied to me just now; to my face. You are just like them. You have become what we are fighting against. This is insanity!"

Gabriella tried to explain herself, but even she didn't understand how she could have ended up with hostages who, she knew, were being tortured. They weren't even getting reliable intel from them. She and Pedro simply didn't know what else to do with them. If they released the hostages, it would undoubtably start trouble. As long as the four men were missing, they could be anywhere and the resistance couldn't be blamed. Gabriella and Pedro had agreed that it is best to detain them for now. The hostages could prove to be useful in a trade, if there were to be a power play.

Gabriella hurried into Miguel's house to collect her belongings. She blasted out the front door storming quickly up the street toward her own childhood home.

Both shoving each other in anger, Miguel continued to argue with Pedro about the hostages. "What else have the two of you had been doing?"

Pedro tried speak soldier to soldier with Gabriella gone, "War is hell, Miguel. Come to your senses. When did anyone promise you they would fight for you but only be nice? You should be proud of Gabriella. She is a strong woman, maybe the strongest I have ever known. She's been working hard and facing problems head on. She isn't afraid of anything except losing. You are too hard on her."

Miguel was confused. He felt betrayed. He would never have considered keeping hostages. It was beneath him. He worried that his men were becoming dishonest, that power and guns were corrupting them, turning them into the very people they were fighting against.

Several hours of talking and arguing had passed when the two men finally relented, both emotionally exhausted. Pedro showered while Miguel began to cook with Maria, who had become subdued of late. Miguel knew she had been unhappy, but he couldn't handle any more and chose to ignore her sadness. He knew this was not the image that she had conjured when she dreamed about living with her mother and Miguel after her wonderful trip to Arizona.

Gabriella did not return for dinner or after, so Pedro offered to go check on her. Miguel wanted to go, but he didn't know how to make the current situation better. He wanted to comfort her, but he was still too angry and confused. It seemed as if Gabriella was just an empty shell of the person he once knew and loved. That shook at his resolve. He didn't understand her or know how to talk to her. One thing he was sure of was that he didn't want to fight again.

***

Pedro was waiting in Gabriella's kitchen, leaning back against the tabletop. Gabriella came into the room wearing a sleeveless cotton top and cotton shorts, looking ready for bed. She was surprised to see him and stood towel drying her hair in the doorway, pausing as she considered what to do with this unexpected guest.

Gabriella was tired of feeling alone and on this night, after arguing with Miguel, she had never been more in need of company. She slowly crossed the room, stopping where he stood. "Pedro, I know we understand each other. You get what I did. You supported me. Now that Miguel knows about the hostages, I feel ashamed. I am afraid that everything Miguel has said about me is true."

Pedro gently pulled Gabriella toward him and she leaned her forehead against his chest. "I think you did the right thing. I think… you are exciting." She reached her hand to touch his waist and let her fingers hold him near his belt. Her other hand was instinctively drawn to the warmth of his body. With her eyes closed Gabriella began to breath in the smell of him, and as her body relaxed, her heart began to pound.

As Pedro's embrace became strong, Gabriella became weak. He bent down, wrapping one powerful arm around her thighs, lifting her off the ground. He slid her thin cotton shirt up in the same motion and dove at her breast like a suckling infant. She gasped but melted against him as pleasure overtook her.

His kisses became soft as he moved slowly up to her neck and mouth. His lips were full and wet and wonderful. Gabriella wrapped her legs around Pedro's hips, grabbing greedily at his strong arms and waist. He turned and sat her on the table. Clothes fell away as their hands explored each other's curves and the softness of golden brown skin.

Pedro was impatient to have her; all of her. He pulled Gabriella close to him as she pressed her thighs open and pushed him inside her. She was impatient too.

With his arm wrapped around her, Pedro held Gabriella as he thrust his hips and pushed inside her again and again. She moaned with pleasure and laid herself back on the table, lost in passion as he caressed her, drinking in her curves. He had recently been making his desire to have her obvious, weakening her resolve. Her hunger for him engulfed her; she had been hoping for a moment like this with him.

Gabriella moaned, arching her back and losing herself in the momentary pleasure of deep satisfying contractions. Pedro listened to her sounds and watched her body tense and fall, as his excitement overtook him. He lay himself over her on the table and wrapped his arms around her like a blanket while they caught their breath.

Pedro began to kiss her again on her shoulder and her neck but Gabriella had turned her face away from him, covering it with her arm. She pressed against him to lift his body off of her. She didn't speak as Pedro stood naked, looking confused before her. She collected her clothes, again briefly resting her forehead on his chest before disappearing into her bedroom. He heard the lock turn.

Pedro slept that night on the living room couch. He wanted to stay, to be near her, but no one else was there to protect her. He couldn't leave her alone. When Gabriella didn't come out of the bedroom in the morning, he knocked softly on her door. She said nothing, and finally he left her alone. Pedro had to face the realization that she craved affection, but his was not the love or approval she truly longed for.

***

The Mayor was careful not to start the engine of his own car. He drank water only from bottles that he purchased himself and carried a gun at all times. Resistance members watched-over his office daily and he knew each of them by name. The police officers were as anxiety ridden as he was. It was hard to know for sure who was working for whom and Mayor kept wondering why he was still alive.

His hair had begun to fall out from constantly stroking it at his temple. He had lost weight in spite of the fact that he was drinking much more. Snorting more coke became normal, too and he wasn't thinking clearly. He called for a meeting with Miguel who agreed to come to his office.

Mayor Ernesto told Miguel that he wasn't sure he would be breathing for long. He said that the cartel had no reason to keep him alive since he was continuing to cooperate with President Desiderio. He said it was only a matter of time before they got to him.

"There was a time, not that long ago, when I felt strong and sure and incorruptible. But, that time had long since passed," he said regretfully.

"I have accepted many bribes during my time in office. I didn't want to at first, I held out, but the cartel didn't leave me with much choice in the matter, if I wanted to live," he continued while rubbing at the dark circles beneath his eyes. "Eventually, I became accustomed to the money. And, it would have stayed that way until you came on the scene."

The Mayor admitted to feeling the pressure to overlook the gang violence, choosing to preserve himself instead of doing the right thing for his community, the very thing that he was hired to do.

"My political ambitions were pure in the beginning," he explained. "I honestly believed I could do something good when I was elected. I beat my opponent by a wide margin," he said with pride. "I guess the people trusted in me. Believe it or not, I once possessed the same passion and vision that you now possess. It makes me ashamed to see how different I am today."

The mayor confessed that while he was afraid to die, he was even more afraid of being tortured. He defended his own cowardly behavior explaining that though he was totally ineffective at his job, the world needed him to serve even if simply as a witness to all the corruption. It was too easy to take the extra money, turn his back and let the cartel run amok. Miguel was sympathetic admitting that he was beginning to understand the blurred lines that good and evil sometimes share.

"I have been keeping a journal of illegal activity, including my own. It is the only worthwhile thing that I could think of to do. The entries have been written separately so that they can be used independently. In other words, you don't have to introduce any evidence until you need it. If the judge sitting on a case is indictable, and he knows it, he will likely do his job honestly knowing you have my reports. Use it to force people back to the good side. This is all I have to offer you.

You should have the cooperation of the corrupt as long as my file exists. President Desiderio is taking advantage of the opportunity you have provided him to regain some power. I have made some audio recordings, too. I am going to be killed at some point, so it is time for me to make an effort to repair some of the damage I have allowed."

He laughed nervously. "I am preparing for my death. I'm worn out and welcome it. But, what I fear most is being tortured. I can barely sleep anymore, thinking about how they are going to treat me. I feel sure that one of these days I will be plucked from of my bed, or worse, my wife will, and then I will find out how much of a coward I really am."

***

The mayor's journal was good news. It would be beneficial to have something to work with besides guns and bullets. Miguel told Pedro, Gabriella and the others that he wanted to turn the hostages over to Maximo as a gesture of peace and good will. However, Miguel was alone in thinking that something good might come of the gesture. Pedro argued that with the hostages, they had some bargaining power. "If we give them back, we will just have four more angry men with a score to settle," Pedro argued.

Miguel did not want to be discovered with the hostages, and now he could use the Mayor's information as a bargaining tool. He decided that he would meet with Maximo in the marketplace and make his final decision there.

14

Confession

They were careful to observe custom of drinking wine and eating together while making small talk like old friends. Maximo admitted that he had been to see the doctor and was told begin taking high blood pressure medicine. He had to lay off the rich foods or cholesterol medicine would be next. He talked about getting older and how troublesome his body's changes were, but that aging was good in some ways because all the years behind him gave him wisdom and understanding of the world. He said it was nice to have time to read and to think. He loved to walk in his garden.

Miguel spoke of the garden he had begun and how the loved the smell of the soil especially when it was wet. He felt healthier when he connected with the soil. He talked about how good it had been to spend time with Maria and that she is a wonderful smart girl who loved going to school and loved making friends. Maximo asked about Gabriella and if they had found their way to being a couple. Miguel answered carefully. He could only think back to the day that Gabriella had learned from Frankie that Maximo had ordered her tortured and then killed. In the back of his mind he always wondered why she had not been attacked.

He was honest and explained that neither of them were comfortable since this unrest. He said that maybe in the future they could relax and enjoy each other. Maximo suggested that perhaps she was more comfortable with Pedro.

Miguel looked at Maximo for a long time without responding. At their last meeting, Maximo suggested that things were not in his control, and they weren't. Miguel had hostages he didn't know about. He wondered if there was something else that he didn't know. Miguel wondered how Maximo might know more than he did about this subject especially. And, why did Maximo keep sneaking information to him. "Maximo, why have you not killed me?"

Maximo smirked. "President Desiderio has ordered that you live, for now. I did not speak to him directly, the message has been passed along through the other families. It is his word to all families that if harm comes to you, he will personally make anyone associated wish they were dead. I am under the impression that he sincerely would like you to live, for now.

It's a bit funny really. Do you know that collectively, there are ten times more people working for the cartels than there are in México's military? It's the truth. I will cooperate with his request for the time being. I am a patient man."

"Why would he protect me?"

"I am sorry to say that you are popular among the people and that killing you will turn you into a martyr. If you die for this cause, the resistance will become stronger instead of weaker. The story of a single man fighting both the cartels and the government spread a message of hope to the weary. I have heard it said that you are seven feet tall and possess Herculean strength. It is better not to strike you down in your prime. Besides, we have already had enough violence. Wouldn't you say?" Miguel wondered if he was joking, but his face showed no hint of it if he was.

Maximo continued, "This war is embarrassing the President internationally. The American media especially is using you to generate ratings. I know I would want punish you for that if I wore his shoes. And in the end, I am sure he will. You embarrassed him in front of the world. If you want to live, you should be careful."

"The world knows what is going on here?"

"Yes, unfortunately. But, don't let it give you false confidence. The world is only minimally interested. The international interest will pass as each country has its own struggles to consider."

"Perhaps with the help of the resistance, President Desiderio would like to have more control over his government and economy." Miguel said. "Maybe he would be proud to have tourism back in México. I have given him the means by which he might achieve these goals." Miguel offered optimistically. "México is known worldwide for the cartels and gang violence. Perhaps you embarrassed him before I did."

"Personally, I don't think it matters. He is a corrupt and greedy man." Maximo said. "He will make a mistake and eventually be his own worst enemy. I can wait while America's media toys with México's President."

Miguel felt that this news put him in a strategically solid position to come clean and made up his mind that he would tell Maximo about the hostages. He had to find the right words.

"Maximo, we have a problem. Some of your men tried to kill the mayor. Did you know about this?"

"I did. And I know they went missing after that."

"Well, I don't want to cause trouble between us. I want to enjoy the peace we have had for a few weeks now." Maximo grinned widely. Miguel didn't understand this response but continued. "I want to tell you where they are. I am hoping that this gesture will be seen as a peaceful one. I understand that having hostages is not right, and that this fact will upset you, but I am not in the hostage business, I am fighting against it so I feel it is important to tell you."

Maximo laughed openly. His eyes twinkled in the sunlight. It was nice to see him laugh and Miguel smiled too, though he didn't know what they were happy about. Maximo shook his head, sipped his wine and chuckled as he gazed upon Miguel with a humored expression.

"You are an honest man, Miguel. An honest man and a fool. Do you think that I don't know where they are?"

"If you know where they are, then why have you not gone to get them?"

"Perhaps, they deserve what they got for not doing the job right."

Miguel fell silent, finally understanding that Maximo had been telling the truth. He did know where the hostages were being held. "All right then, I won't bother to divulge where they are."

"Tell me you have a greater purpose for meeting today than that."

Stunned, Miguel felt foolish as an urgent need to get away overtook him. He quickly downed his wine before saying his formal goodbye.

He marched across the plaza heading toward his car, his eyes cast to the cobblestone. He was beginning to think that Maximo was playing with him like a cat plays with a mouse before devouring it. The cat mirthfully swats at it allowing the mouse scamper a distance toward liberty but then knife like claws pierce its skin. The mouse weakens with each strike, but eventually dies of stress, much to the cat's disappointment. Miguel wondered if stress would be Maximo's strongest tool, but could almost feel the sting of sharp claws.

The unmistakable boom of gunfire echoed twice throughout the marketplace. People glanced at one another but moved like a wave away from the origin of the sound until Miguel stood alone. He saw Maximo hesitate and then enter his car before driving away.

Miguel was compelled to go to the source, a storefront belonging to a merchant that he had armed.

The owner recognized Miguel upon entering, lowering his weapon, he begged for help. "They are just boys, Miguel! Boys—came to collect the taxes. I didn't know what to do. They were breaking my merchandise. They wouldn't fire, but they wouldn't leave. Help me."

"I will get my car and we can carry them out. Wrap them in something. I'll be right back." Miguel's head began to spin with confused thoughts and emotions. He knew what needed to be done, and like having been set to autopilot, his body was doing it, but his thoughts betrayed him. These were teenage boys and he was going to hide their lifeless bodies. Their mother's would soon have broken hearts, but first they would worry. In what way is this not as bad as keeping hostages? In what way is this not as evil as cartel behavior?

***

The morning the news reported:

"Four men were recovered this morning in poor condition from a cement building commonly referred to as the "Gates of Hell" in el pueblo de Esperanza after an anonymous caller notified local police. It has been alleged that Miguel Garces and his militante de la Resistencia, named as a symbol of their strength, El valiente guerreros, the brave warriors, is responsible for kidnapping these men. Señor Garces has refused to comment, however, he is expected be interrogated by police and charged for this crime later today. The men are in poor condition and being treated at the local La flor de la Esperanza hospital.

Señor Garces' coup has been watched but tolerated by local police while they played the role of Robin Hood, taking from the wealthy cartels and giving to the poor. It is unknown what the fall out will be throughout the community of Esperanza and beyond upon realization that this movimiento de resistencia is not the savior they claimed it be, but instead both dangerous and hypocritical, participating in the very actions they criticize. La pregunta grande que people are asking today is: Are people safe with this new savage gang running rampant?"

***

"This is crazy. What the hell is he doing?" Miguel hated being called a savage gang. Public disgrace felt worse than he imagined it would. People had looked up to him, and he felt the full burden and responsibility of it. He wanted them to be safe, but he felt as though he was losing control. And, he worried that things would soon be worse if he didn't plan his next move.

Gabriella had begged Miguel to keep quiet about the hostages. "I told you it was a bad idea. Now what are we going to do?" Gabriella's hostility came as an equally painful surprise. "There is bound to be a retaliation."

"Maximo knew. He already knew, Gabriella. I didn't tell him where they were. I only told him that we had them. He has just been playing with us. It doesn't make sense. I have to talk to him again. I have to figure out what he knows and how he knows it. I need to find out why he is doing this."

Pedro said. "It was nothing more than a public relations stunt. He is attempting to turn the public against you. If he can ruin your reputation and make your people turn away from you, they will accept his terms much easier. You have given people hope. For him, that is more dangerous than weapons. If he can make them think you are more evil than he is, they will want him over you.

The resistance will dissolve, his problem goes away and it is back to business as usual."

Miguel knew all along that Maximo had been stopping the Mexican media from reporting any news he sent to them, especially good news. He didn't realize that at the same time, Maximo was plotting to use the media against him. It was a move that Miguel didn't see coming. Miguel worried that public opinion may be the most dangerous weapon Maximo could have used. When the people no longer trust Miguel, it will be the beginning of the end.

"I need to talk to him. More importantly, I need him to talk to me. Let's plan to host *la comida,* lunch feast; like in the old days. I am going to invite Maximo." Miguel said Santino had been a brutal, passionate leader with a bad temper. Maximo was different. It was harder to know what to expect from him. Miguel had not considered the possibility of an intellectual battle with the cartel. "I need to spend some time with him. He is in my head. It's time for me to discover what he is all about. I don't have another play."

As long as President Desiderio held the moratorium on killing Miguel, Miguel had the advantage. It was time to begin planning two things; how to keep the resistance relevant and how to stay alive if Maximo was the worthy opponent it appeared that he was. He wondered how it could be that he was preparing his mind for retreat as well as for success. He also wondered how he had come this far without either of these preparations being ready.

Miguel noticed that Gabriella wasn't spending much time with Pedro. She avoided eye contact and didn't say much either. She simply didn't seem comfortable. Usually, they agreed on everything. They had become so close that Miguel had begun to feel envious and uneasy. Something had changed between them. Miguel wondered if it was just Maximo influencing his thoughts or if there was something he needed to know about the pair.

Miguel hated being associated with the hostage taking. He couldn't imagine a scenario where that would be something he would do. He felt anger toward Gabriella and Pedro. But, hoped it wasn't obvious. He didn't want to deepen the ever expanding rift growing between them.

Pedro hung up his phone and announced that Maximo's plan was working against him. He said, "The families of the four imprisoned men were mouthing off, displaying their bruises and making threats in town, but everyone was glad to see that Miguel was not afraid to make the cartel suffer the same way that so many of their own families had suffered."

"I don't want him here." Gabriella said.

"I don't see how it could hurt us." Papi said. "He will relax more here than in town with everyone watching. If we're going to get any information out of him, he has to be relaxed."

"We certainly can't go to him." Pedro said.

15

Games

Miguel paced like an expectant father while awaiting Maximo's arrival. He tried to remember why he had thought it was a good idea to invite this particular man into his home.

It was beginning to feel like home again for Miguel. Maria and Gabriella had become quite comfortable as well. The three had begun to sleep at Miguel's house regularly, and occasionally Papi, *Abuela* or Pedro stayed there too.

Miguel's hands had lovingly cleaned and straightened the family photos on the wall. He fluffed pillows and generally fidgeted. He snapped at Maria for having left her school books under foot. No one usually minded because it made them feel like a normal family, but today was different. *Abuela* tried to persuade Miguel to help in the kitchen, but he was clumsy and distracted so she sent him away again, "Soaking beans in water is not that difficult, Miguel. Go!"

He pulled back the curtain at the window and stared at the yard. The motionless flag drooped toward the ground from the pole Miguel had installed. Cars had been driving passed the house all morning. Miguel was sure they were scanning the area to ensure Maximo's safety, but it only added to his nervousness.

It was Maria who finally settled Miguel with a hug. She squeezed herself into the space between his body and the window and wrapped her arms around him. He was still distracted, but in her arms he remembered simple pleasure of being loved. Her warm embrace seemed to calm him. "I'm sorry I lost my patience with you."

"It's okay, Papa. You have a great deal on your mind today."

"How did you get to be so smart?"

Maria smiled as he kissed her forehead.

The aroma of garlic, cumin, onion and oregano wafted from the kitchen. Papi said, "Our guest better be on time, or I am starting without him." Then he laughed. "Everything smells great. May I have a taste?" he asked but his fingers had already pinched a bit of pollo, from the pan.

"Get out of here" *Abuela* slapped the wooden spoon on the counter as a warning. "You're an animal. Go sweep the porch or something." The familiar smells, the racket of Papi begging for samples, and sounds of dishes being readied made the absence of Miguel's mother painfully significant. He wondered how many more times his heart could break simply by remembering her. He kept expecting a playful, soiled, seven year old Juan Carlos to come blasting in the door. Miguel didn't want to forget them; he just wanted his chest to stop squeezing him like a vice every time they came to mind.

Maximo arrived without all the extra security like in the marketplace. This surprised but pleased Miguel. He was driven by Marcos who stepped out of the car and then turned to help Maximo. Miguel remembered seeing Marcos at the club. He recalled watching Marcos as he tracked Maria while she moved about Santino's club.

Maximo was introduced to Gabriella, Maria, *Abuela* and Pedro, but he kissed the cheeks of Padre Cayo, saying that he was happy to have him back in the church where he belonged. Everyone exchanged quizzical glances when they heard him say this. After all, Padre Cayo's return was solely due to the fact that the organ harvesting business had been shut down.

The gifts of wine and sweet treats that Maximo had brought were distributed, while Marcos made his way through the house unescorted. Maximo presented matching gold bracelets to Maria and Gabriella. He apologized to *Abuela*, promising something for her next time. She smiled and nodded. She understood most of what he had said, though she relied on lip reading as much as hearing. She thanked him, "The wine was a lovely gift," as she headed to the kitchen with the bottles.

Gabriella asked Marcos if he would be joining them for lunch. He was slow to realize that the group had been watching as he stood staring at Maria. The room had become silent until he shook himself from the trance and excused himself saying, "Next time. Thanks." Before exiting, he mumbled to Maximo, "I'll be back for you."

Everyone settled onto the patio with a cool drink of iced tea, but conversation was awkward at best until Maria invited Maximo to play a game of chess with her. While surprised, both Gabriella and Miguel smile at each other. "Children have a way of simplifying matters." Miguel said. "Their lack of bias enables them to make friends easily." Maximo agreed to play, and Maria carried the board over to where he was sitting.

They began setting the pieces up. Maria asked if he would like to be white, giving him the opportunity to make the first move. He declined, so Maria made the first play with her pawn. It was a beginner's opening move. Maria looked up with wide eyes to meet his, which had narrowed. This made her laugh.

Maximo looked like somebody's *abuelo* to her, and she treated him as such. She would steal glances at this powerful, fearsome man, man in charge of the cartel families in the area, a man who controlled life and death, who wrote and rewrote local history, as they animated the rigid lifeless pieces in a slow dance around the board. She tried to observe what was so unique about him that would make him so formidable. Why was he different from other people?

She didn't notice any distinction. He was old, she thought. He breathed air, like she did. He showed apprehension; she thought he wanted to win the game as much as she did. With every piece she moved, he would nod his head in approval or narrow his eyes in concern. He would look into her wide eyes and then grin. He was trying to read her face, but all she revealed was youth and beauty, eagerness and patience. He was trying to understand her moves, perhaps afraid she might have the advantage.

The two were so engaged in the game that the others excused themselves one by one until Maximo and Maria were left alone together. She said, "I have been watching your face, which I like. You don't seem scary. I think you look smart, but you worry. Your eyebrows are always pushed close to your eyes. Why do you worry so much?"

"At the moment I am worried that I will be beaten by a child," Maximo admitted.

"What would it mean if I beat you at a silly game of chess?"

"It would mean that you are smart and skilled, and that I may have left my best days in my past. No one wants to face the fact that the end of their time on earth is closer than the beginning."

He paused to stare at the pieces. "We all fear death, but not only because it is death. We fear it because of the loss of life. I know I would like to have more moments like this one where a lovely, smart girl sits across from me demonstrating her wit and skill, showing me what is beautiful about life and learning."

"If you understand these things, things like what it is like to be scared, why do you deliberately cause so many people to be afraid?"

His focus changed from the game to Maria as he sat back. "That is a fair question. But, let me ask you a question first. What do you think would happen if I stopped doing business? What would happen if I told everyone who works for me that we will no longer sell drugs?"

"I think someone else would sell them."

"That's right. As long as people want to use drugs, someone will sell drugs. People are inherently good and often need a reason to be bad. But, when given a reason, many have the ability to be very bad. I cannot change this truth. It has existed since the beginning of time. So, is it really me you should be afraid of or should you be afraid of what people will do for money?"

"I am a little afraid of both," she said while carefully examining the board.

"Many great men and women have tried to break the cycle, to convince people to do good deed instead of bad, and many people have improved their behavior as a result. Do you know about Mother Theresa, Gandhi, Malayla? Even your Miguel."

"Why do you want to hurt him then, if you know he is trying to do the right thing?" Maria asked.

She could see that Maximo was losing his patience for her line of questioning.

"I am not trying to hurt Miguel. I am a businessman. I have to protect my own business. If the government protected its people with the same passion that I run my business, there would only be room for one of us, and the winner would be the government and maybe then the people.

But, people are corruptible. They think about how they can make their life better without considering how their small indiscretions will affect other people and then society as a whole. It's called Individualism. Given the smallest fissure, evil will grow. And that is what has happened here in México."

"Did you just call yourself evil then?" Maria asked.

Maximo's face became severe, showing all the darkness within his heart. "Maria, I will forgive your rudeness this time because I know you are not familiar with entertaining guests. Please, do not push me to impatience. We have only just met. You might consider letting the men discuss important matters."

Maria looked ashamed, and her cheeks blushed. Her next words came out as though they had been glued inside her mouth. Finally she managed, "I'm sorry that I was rude."

Maximo nodded his approval. "Life is a great gift, Maria. Survival is a privilege earned by those who are unafraid to do what needs to be done. Let me tell you a story. Do you know that some ants pull the legs off of other creatures like crickets? Then they drag them into their lair, an underground labyrinth, where all light and sound disappears." He watched her face as he spoke.

"Their victim is alive and aware and remains that way until the ant reaches the deepest depths of the last tunnel, the coldest place in the nest. This is where the ant drops the poor creature to wait, for what, it does not know.

There it lays in pain, unable to move without legs, in darkness, away from its family and friends and the warmth of the sun. It lays in cold storage until the day the colony needs food. I imagine that it welcomes death on that day, Maria.

Now, are you angry at the ant? Or, do you respect the ant like I do for being clever enough to have found a way to survive and even thrive. The hungry ant can't think about what is nice. It simply does what needs to be done to survive."

Maria didn't respond out of fear that her response would be called rude again. Maximo's face had frightened her as much as his story. She kept her eyes on the board. "Why are you trying to scare me?"

"This is life, Maria. Even ants have to eat. They have other worries too, you know. They have wars. They fight other colonies who dare to cross into their territory. These territorial boundaries are important. Within these boundaries their population grows based on the resources that lay within. They must protect their territory to ensure their survival.

So, how do they do that? They send the oldest ants out into combat first followed directly by the rest of the colony. The oldest ants have experience, and the younger ants learn the art of war from them. They learn to be brave and to sacrifice themselves when necessary for the benefit of the group. Have you figured out how they fight?" Maria shook her head. "They pull the legs off of the other ants.

When the ants run for the border to protect it, they know they will suffer the same fate that they have imposed on so many others. Whether they think that separating a creature from its limbs is cruel or not is hard to know, but they understand the most basic law of nature. They have learned that it is the right of the fittest to survive."

Maria listened carefully, and it was clear that the story caused her to feel sad, but she remained quiet. It was hard to know what to say or how to fully understand Maximo's message.

"But, it is an unchangeable truth. We were made with the ability to be evil, and we are all corruptible. You will see that corruption has ruined every great nation throughout history. Corruption itself either bankrupts the economy or it leaves the nation weak enough for a predator to conquer it. In either case, ironically, no one wins. People don't care what the name of the leader is, they simply want to feed their families and be safe.

"Is it so unusual for a young person to want a change? I want to change things, but how can I?"

"I don't know the answer to that. I know that when people come together, greatness can be achieved. Pyramids are build, rocket ships land on the moon, diseases are cured. I believe that the power of prayer has caused miracles." Maximo selected one of his pieces and moved it. "Dedicate yourself to learning. An educated culture is an inspired culture. Believe in a divine power, no matter what you call it. It gives hope to the hopeless. Pray, but know that human nature will not change."

"I don't believe you. People change. We just have to do it together. I will pray for peace. I know what to do. I will write a letter to Malala, she is a girl like me, but she had to fight against the Taliban. I will ask her for guidance. She is also working for peace in her region of the world. I will do the same."

Maximo smiled and reached across the board to touch Maria's face. His smile changed to a frown and then hers did as well. "What's the matter?" she asked.

"You are as ambitious as your Miguel. I don't know what to do about you. Maria, let's finish this game another day."

***

Maximo loved to eat. He treated every morsel as though it were perfection. He loved to tell stories and to laugh. At times Miguel had to remind himself that this man was not family. He was a dangerous man.

After dinner, Miguel and Maximo left the table to walk a bit, allowing Maximo to light up a cigar. For Maximo, these two things were as much a part of the meal as the food and wine. He pulled the cigar from his pocket, brought it to his nose and drew a long breath while his eyes dropped closed. He wetted it in his mouth and bit off a small piece of the end, rolling it in his fingers and inhaling its sweet aroma again. Miguel waited and watched the routine in wonder.

It became obvious to Miguel that Maximo took the time to truly enjoy whatever he was doing. He lived in the moment, attentive and appreciative. Miguel didn't want to spoil the sensuous experience Maximo was enjoying, so he remained quiet, waiting patiently. Maximo dug around in his pocket until he produced a thin box of wooden matches. Miguel wondered why he made such a rudimentary choice when a lighter would be more reliable and convenient. He would ask Maximo this question one day. After a few puffs, Maximo began to walk again, seeming to formulate the next topic in his mind.

They walked out of the yard and started down the road. Miguel was inclined to make excuses for the condition into which his neighbors' homes had fallen. Most of the buildings stood empty, boldly wearing the signs of neglect. He didn't know how to explain that these places were once beautiful until the owners had gone missing or escaped. Maximo didn't seem to notice. He strolled at his ease as though he were surrounded by opulence.

"I have spent a great deal of time thinking about you lately, Miguel. I am sure that comes as no surprise. I have found a way for us to work together. A way to not be enemies. How would you feel about becoming mayor?"

"I had not considered it. We already have a mayor."

"This might be a good time for you to tell the people that you will become mayor, if anything should happen to him. Or, when his term is up. I will not oppose you. I will not challenge it or recommend my own candidate. I would actually support you."

"Why would I do this? And, why would you support me?" Miguel spoke incredulously.

"You would be wise to remember that you are either with me or against me. It would be better for everyone if you took up a government position, and we worked together. A great deal could be accomplished for both of us if you accepted this role. The people will want you to be their official leader instead of the resistance leader. A man with your reputation could easily win an election. You could then work from an official capacity."

"What is in it for you, Maximo?"

"It is a good business move for me. It will be good for my image to show support for you and what you have accomplished."

Miguel was stunned. He felt much like a pawn from the chess board to which Maximo had earlier been so attentive. He hoped that Maria, at least, had been better at figuring out what Maximo's next moves would be. "I'll think about it and talk to Gabriella, but I have a question for you. Why didn't you retrieve your men if you knew that we had take them and where we were keeping them?"

"As I told you before, they deserved what they got. They should have done the job correctly."

"Why did you get the media involved?"

"Because it benefitted me to do so."

"But, the townspeople were glad that we took the hostages. How did that benefit you?"

"I am a businessman. I have no obligation to tell you everything. Be patient. Not everything needs to be revealed at one time."

***

Abuela and Gabriella found their way to the kitchen to clean. "I remember when you were a girl, you never came in the kitchen and did dishes with the women. Do you remember? You were so in love with Miguel that you would both sneak off and think that no one missed you. Where did you go?" Gabriella smiled, but did not answer. "Come on. Tell your secrets. We are both grown women now and there should be nothing hidden between us." Gabriella continued to clear the dishes silently and didn't tell any secrets.

"What is wrong, Gabriella?"

"Nothing. Nothing is wrong."

"I don't believe you. I may not hear very well, but I can see, you know? I can see that something is different between you and Miguel. You don't look in each other's eyes. He is not leaning back in his chair to stroke your leg like he used to. Do you remember? You thought we didn't know, but we all knew. We knew because we did the same things when we were young. We did the same things." *Abuela* laughed a warm, hardy laugh. "Those were happy times. We were so happy for you both. It was nice to have romance in the house. It was nice to know we would be family someday."

Gabriella stopped drying the dishes and put her face in her hands. She began to cry. *Abuela* stopped washing too, as though she had expected this reaction, dried her hands and took Gabriella in her arms. She held Gabriella and stroked her hair.

Gabriella wrapped her arms around *Abuela's* thick waist, relieved to be held like a child, and let herself be rocked and patted. She rested her head on *Abuela's* shoulder and waited. She wanted to stay there forever feeling, safe and protected. It had been half her lifetime since she had felt this safe and at home.

"I miss those days, *Abuela*, very thing was so simple. I miss feeling like Miguel loved me."

"Okay, that's enough now. It's time to stop crying and speak the truth. The truth will ease your mind."

Gabriella took a minute to find her voice, "*Abuela*, I have done some terrible, horrible things. I am so ashamed. I cannot even believe what I have done lately. At the time, it felt right. I felt strong. I felt that I had no choice, but now my actions haunt me. Padre Cayo has absolved me of my sins, and I have prayed to be forgiven. But, it doesn't help. The worst of it is that Miguel is ashamed of me. He doesn't love me anymore. How could he? I am a monster."

Abuela soothed her, "Gabriella, you should not be ashamed of fighting against bad men. Someone had to be strong enough to face the problems we have had. You have done so much good. Maria can go to school now because of your courage. You are free again, and all those captive children are finding their way home. The men that you killed would have killed you if you had not been brave enough to do what had to be done. I am proud of you, my dear. I always thank God that you are here with us, with Miguel, and that you are brave."

Abuela reached out to grasp Gabriella's shoulders, looking her in the eyes, "I think you are wrong about Miguel. He still loves you. He will always love you. Do you know he has never been in love with anyone but you? That's what he told me. I think he always knew in his heart that he would find you, and you would be together.

Loving is easier than you think, my dear. This is just a hard time. Ease your mind. You put too much pressure on yourself. You did your best. Forgive yourself, and move on. Nothing is ever perfect. Look for the small miracles, my dear. Let love into your heart and everything will be beautiful again. I promise that there is something beautiful to be found in every day."

**

Marcos was waiting in the car for Maximo. Miguel carefully kept his hand under Maximo's elbow as he guided him out to the driveway and into the car. They shook hands and agreed to meet again. "How about next Sunday? I know Maria is looking forward to finishing your game." Miguel urged. Although he thought it a strange feeling to take such care assisting a man who might order him killed before he made it to the end of the driveway.

"Maria is looking forward to winning our game," Maximo said with a laugh. "Fine. Next Sunday. We can talk more business, about our plans for the future."

After the two men had driven away, Miguel, Gabriella, Papi, Pedro, *Abuela* and Padre Cayo gathered at the dining room table to discuss the events of the afternoon.

"The good news is that you are safe," Pedro said. "I don't think Maximo is lying. Miguel's existence is somehow beneficial right now. We just have to figure out how to keep it that way. I do think he is definitely setting you up, though. Maximo is a patient man and much smarter than Santino was. I feel like he has a plan that we can't yet see. I'd also like to know if we are safe as well or just you!"

"Are you going to accept his offer and take the job?" Gabriella asked.

"For the moment, we still have a mayor," Miguel said. "But, if I did ever accept the job, all of you would have to obey the laws.

Can you even imagine what that would be like? I would be expected to prosecute you. How awful it would be to end your rein of terror," he said sarcastically.

"That's not funny," Gabriella said.

"Maybe that's what he wants," Pedro said. "Maybe he wants to turn us against each other. It's an interesting play on his part."

"Right now," Papi added, "Maximo has to fight against the resistance and the government. I don't see what we, well, the resistance, stands to gain from you becoming the mayor."

"I'm sure he is thinking that once you are in office, he will have more control over you. One decision at a time, he will force you to compromise until you are working for him anyway," Pedro explained. "He is thinking that the resistance will dissolve without you at its leader. And, he's probably right." Pedro then revealed that men had been complaining. The same men who had been working, year after year, at the back breaking job of migrant workers were now upset because they didn't receive an SUV. They said they needed SUVs to patrol areas.

Miguel wondered, "How could greed have set in so quickly?"

Pedro said, "Obviously, a car would make things easier for everyone, but there are so many men now. We couldn't fill the orders if we had a dealership."

"What about the weapons?"

"We are out pretty much out of weapons. We issued some to other areas, and now there's nothing left. We have explosives, if that makes you feel any better."

Pedro had witnessed the chaos from his third floor recon room and had recorded some of it. He had saved some of the highlights and promised to show them to Miguel. Friction and unrest were still breaking out between the police, the cartelistas, as well as the resistance. Sometimes it was hard to tell who the good guys were.

Pedro continued, "There's a lot of arguing, Miguel. Too much. I'm beginning to wonder if some men have been selling their weapons and then asking for more. We don't have more. That news is bound to make it back to Maximo. Others have complained that they are out of cash and need to go find work. In many ways, it feels like the beginning of the end."

Miguel said, "Why do you have to talk like that? Let's just stay positive. We have no choice."

Pedro tried to joke, "So, now we're arguing. Great. See, I can be positive. I said great."

The resistance was struggling in spite of the fact that there were so many men. No one had an accurate count of how many there really were. This was good for many reasons, but so much harder to manage. Cliques had begun to break off and band together into smaller, more effective gang-like clusters.

But, there was good news too. Local businesses were beginning to show a profit or at least were able to pay off some debt now that they were not paying taxes to the cartel. This enabled owners to hire a few, men but mostly they were fixing up their stores and reinvesting in their businesses. The town was slowly coming back to life.

***

The morning news station reported:

"Señor Maximo Trejo announced plans today to build a beverage manufacturing factory on recently purchased land on the outskirts of el pueblo de Esperanza. This will provide local builders and craftsmen much needed employment opportunities. And, once the project is complete, he hopes to employ one thousand people inside the manufacturing plant.

Señor Trejo states that he is pleased to be able to help the hard working citizens of Esperanza. El pueblo de Esperanza was his own home as a child. Señor Trejo is happy to know the folks from his hometown will not be forced to travel great distances on unsafe buses like they are forced to do now."

***

The reporter then interviewed several townspeople who expressed their sincere appreciation to Señor Trejo. They were, "Grateful to God and grateful to Señor."

Miguel concluded that Maximo had figured out a way to get his narcotics into the beverage containers. That was obvious. What he didn't understand was why the "show"? The insult to the government busing was blatant antagonizing. Why was he putting on a display of caring for the local people? Miguel was beginning to anticipate the next *la comida* with Maximo. Clearly, Maximo had been busy making plans. Miguel wondered why Maximo hadn't shared his good news last week when they so much time together. He was becoming intimidated by Maximo's liberal use of the media and wondered if Maximo was capable of fine tuning an image and using the media to market that image. Like a fly buzzing close to his face, the thought kept taunting him. Miguel shuddered as he pondered what Maximo might have arranged to happen next.

16

Decisions

Sunday was becoming a day to look forward to, a welcomed interruption in the hostilities. Miguel's house came alive with meal preparations and the wonderful aromas of Mexican spices and American foods. Maria helped *Abuela* work in the kitchen while listening to her stories. She learned the proper way to slice an onion, but also learned about Juan Carlos and Mama. *Abuela's* heart had kept them alive and well; she spoke of them as though they would be joining in the feast. Miguel loved collecting the remnants of his family under one roof for *la comida*, much like when he was young.

Maximo had accepted Miguel's invitation as though he had expected it. Unfortunately, everyone had forgotten about Marcos until he stepped out of the car to assist Maximo. Maximo said he hoped it wouldn't be a problem if Marcos joined them for the afternoon. It was hastily decided that Marcos would stay, and Maria's face turned white.

Maximo began passing out the gifts he had brought. Maria had been especially pleased with hers, a pretty white dress with soft lace falling in layers.

"When could I ever wear such a pretty dress?" she asked.

"Why not wear it today? It would please me if you would wear it today." Maximo suggested. She smiled and ran off to change her clothes.

When Maria returned the room fell silent in awe. Gabriella felt tears damped her cheeks though she wore a small smile on her lips. Marcos squirmed in his chair until he sat with all the height he could stretch into. Miguel stepped back to hide his furrowed brow while trying to comprehend the reason for Maximo to select this gift. Maximo, Miguel had learned, had a reason for everything he did. The high neck, lace and bows emphasized the tenderness of Maria's age, yet somehow, to him, she also looked the part of a child bride. Maria's sought Miguel's approval, and he forced a smile, exclaiming that he had never seen anything so beautiful.

Maximo nodded to Maria with satisfaction saying, "I see only the angel that you are in that white dress. I hope I will always remember you as you are today." Maria flew to him and wrapped her arms around his neck in a tight hug. He chuckled and stepped back so that his eyes could meet hers. "You are no use in the kitchen wearing white. Perhaps you could walk for a while with Marcos." Marcos stood up, placing his hand on her back as though guiding her toward the door.

Maria's head dropped in disappointment, but she responded to the power of Maximo's suggestion like a puppet on a string. The dread she had felt upon Marcos arrival had everything to do with this moment.

Miguel stood in their path to the door until Maximo assured him, "Marcos knows he is not to stray beyond our sight." Stepping aside reluctantly, Miguel wished he could see Maria's eyes as the two left the house to walk.

Once outside, Marcos asked Maria how she had been, adding that he missed seeing her each night at the club. He boldly proclaimed that she was the only beautiful thing in the club. Maria recoiled at his confidence. He had changed somehow in the short time they had not seen each other. She had known he had spent most of his evenings at the club watching her, but he rarely tried to speak to her, and flirting had never been allowed.

The clear social boundaries of their relationship had comforted her. Maria had been afraid of Marcos because she knew that one day she would be forced to marry someone and had guessed that it might be him. But, she had also been comforted by his attention. She secretly looked forward to it. Other than his admiring eyes, she would go weeks at a time without feeling noticed by anyone.

Maria asked about her club friends, and Marcos assured her that they missed her as well. He offered to come by another day and drive her back to the club for a visit. Maria instantly perked up and looked at Marcos's face for the first time. He looked away.

Maria studied the man beside her for a moment. She could see that he was nervous and seemed younger somehow. From his profile, she could see his long, brown eye lashes which furnished his face with a softness that she had always enjoyed. His lips curled upward slightly at the corners, giving him the appearance of an optimist; she liked that too. His long slender fingers, with their manicured nails, left no hint that they were capable of violence. For the first time, in the safety of Miguel's family home, Maria allowed herself to relax for a moment and notice how handsome Marcos was. She knew he was going to turn twenty-one soon, but he seemed suddenly more youthful, and this pleased her.

Their stroll led them first to the hammock. They both paused in front of it, but then Maria pointed to a swinging bench just beyond it saying, "Miguel likes to come outside and sit by himself in the yard. He says that we should all make peace with ourselves in this way, that inside a quiet mind you will find the voice of reason. This voice tells the truth if you find the courage to listen. It doesn't tell you what you want to hear. It makes you aware of what you already know, but wish you didn't. Miguel says the voice will always resonate, like all of the other sounds, in the background of our lives. We have to tune into it and be unafraid of what it says in order to find peace. He says that no matter what state of chaos the world is in, the burden will be less if you have listened to the voice inside yourself."

"Miguel sounds like a smart man. Maximo speaks that way too except it's a little more complicated." Marcos said.

"I had a chance to talk with Maximo the last time he came over, and I agree. His inner voice is a little darker than Miguel's."

She slid her foot to the ground and gently pushed the bench which began to move. Marcos lifted his feet forcing him to sit back and hold them awkwardly above the ground. They sat in silence enjoying the peace of the afternoon. He rested his heels, slowing the rocking until it stopped.

Without looking at Maria he asked, "That night in the club, that night when my father was killed just outside the parking lot, did you know what was happening?" He spoke carefully with tension in his voice. Maria began to feel frightened again. She was sure he didn't want to hear the answer and couldn't understand why he would ask it. She hoped that this was the only difficult question his inner voice had instructed him to ask her.

The truth was that she didn't know that Marcos's father would be killed that night. All she knew that night was that something was going to happen and that she should be on guard. But, she considered lying and telling Marcos that she did know. This would make him hate her, and then she could be free of him. But, she didn't really want him to hate her either though.

"That night was the worst night of my life." Marcos continued. "It was the worst night because my father was murdered. But, what added to that pain was that the girl who I loved, the girl who I had planned to marry may have known about the plot and distracted me so that I couldn't have saved my father. I want to know if you tricked me into staying at the club. I thought I was protecting you. I need to know if you made a fool of me."

Guilt and sadness overwhelmed Maria. She instinctively reached for him and touched his arm, "I am sorry for your loss,

Marcos." Since that evening, she had not even thought about Marcos or how his life had been devastated on the same night that she had become free. The long pause that followed was enough that it seemed as if they both had forgotten his question.

When Marcos finally turned to Maria a tear had formed and sat balanced on those beautiful lashes as though awaiting the perfect moment to roll dramatically down his cheek. "But maybe, Maria, maybe you knew and you kept me there to protect me from the same fate. Is that what you did? Did you protect me? I have been hoping that now that you will be fourteen, you see me as a man who you can love, as I see the woman in you." Her hand flew from his arm. "I can't go another day without seeing you. I am moving up in the business, and it is time for me to take a wife. It is expected." Marcos lifted her hands in his own and lowered himself to one knee. Maria's heart began to thump wildly, and she tried to pull her hands away. Marcos held on and quickly asked with a sob and streaming tears, "Will you marry me?"

Maria pulled herself away and tired to run for the house. Marcos jerked her back. "You have been promised to me. You have to marry me." He pulled her close and kissed her. It wasn't the soft kiss of new lovers. It was the hard, aggressive kiss of an experienced man. She pierced her lips tightly closed and began to thump her fists on his arms. He was strong and determined; she had no effect.

Suddenly outside, Miguel yelled to Marco, and he let go. They stood facing each other, both panting until Maria shouted tearfully, "I am only thirteen. I want to go to college someday. You have no patience. I have a choice! You should have been patient." She stormed off toward the house with her pretty white dress bouncing along with her steps. She shouted at Maximo as she passed, "I hate you and your stupid dress!"

Maximo appeared genuinely hurt but let Maria go and sauntered slowly toward Marcos, who was clearly having trouble regaining his composure. The two men walked outside until dinner was ready and then they rejoined the group. Maria remained in her room.

Marcos was unsettled, and apologized for disturbing their afternoon. He glanced so often at Maria's closed door that it seemed more a nervous tick than a conscious decision.

***

After dinner Maximo and Miguel left the house for their walk, the two men stepping in a familiar stride. Neither rushed to speak. Both had a mind full of thoughts that needed to be expressed but both knew that once spoken, things would change forever. Neither was willing to sacrifice this moment to rancor.

"Marcos is not welcome here anymore." Miguel began.

Maximo had no visible reaction to Miguel's words. "You worry too much." Maximo responded. "He is a good man. Have you never found it difficult to resist the urge to kiss the woman you love?" Miguel was silent as both men knew that he struggled with this thought daily.

"I have never forced my will upon a woman. That is where he crossed the line. And, she's not a woman. She's a girl."

"Miguel, we are only here for a short time. Live in the moment. Find some peace. You are so worried about yesterday and tomorrow that you never even enjoy today. Be in the moment. Be happy for the gift that this moment is."

Miguel wondered how Maximo could dismiss Marcos's actions so easily. He wondered how Maximo had come to know his mind so well, so quickly. Miguel wished that he possessed the same ability. "What would Marcos have done if we were not watching?" Miguel asked.

"The boy is in love, Miguel. He would not have hurt Maria. Santino had promised to save Maria for him. It was a bargain struck years before this by his father. He feels like a man whose juicy pig roast jumped up from his plate and ran away when he poked it with his fork. Know this, *mi amigo*; his heart is set. Maria will have to come around to the idea in time. You will be wise to know this. Now, enough of that for tonight."

Miguel stopped walking. His head was dizzy. A sense of panic began to set in. He could see that Maximo's mouth was moving, but he no longer heard the words. How dare he make such a threat, Miguel thought. He looked back to the house and saw Maria back in her colorful outfit, brooding over the chess set with a plate of dinner beside her. He hoped that meant that Marcos had finally left.

Maximo puffed his cigar and waited for Miguel to recover. "As I was saying, when you become mayor, we will succeed in get things done. It will be a good partnership. We will get things done because you are a reasonable man. A fair man. I understand what is in your heart." He puffed again on the cigar and Miguel watched the tip blaze red.

"The President is making things tough on anyone who harvests anything other than crops. Now, this is affecting my income, but it is a good thing. That was a nasty business. And, it means that you have what you wanted." Maximo stopped speaking to remove a piece of tobacco from his mouth with his fingertips.

"We will work together to find a balance for all other businesses. We will compromise. When the new beverage factory is ready, those who wish to work, will seek employment there. Those who desire more excitement and more money will enter one of my other enterprises. You will be protected for as long as we are working together. Gabriella and Maria will fall under that protection as well. I know you mean well, and so it pleases me to know you will live."

It was hard to know how to feel about this proposition. Miguel had come to the realization that, after all of this struggle, he would end up working for the cartel. That had not changed. He would do the cartel's bidding, or he would be killed. Miguel guessed that he was the only man ever to be told twice; "You are either with or against me." Gabriella and Maria would still be hostages of sorts, and their safety would be completely dependent upon his cooperation. He found himself wondering what had been gained after so much effort.

This conversation made Miguel feel the same tightness in his gut as his conversation with Santino right before he began organizing the resistance movement. This time, though, there were no more cards to play. Maximo might as well have said "checkmate."

"Maximo, I cannot be mayor under your terms. You expect me to promote your businesses. It's a trap. You will pick and pick until I am completely corrupted and serve only you. You will be charming and grandfatherly to Maria and earn her trust. But, I will know that you are in fact keeping her near so that you can manipulate me with the treat of killing her.... or worse."

"Miguel, you are a good man. You had the right idea to free the women you love and rescue the captive kids. But, you are a fool to fight the tides. I don't believe that you have given this conversation enough time. Think this through. What other option do you have?

You think that you are fighting against me, but you are mistaken. It is the will of the people you need to fight. You have done well. We have peace for the moment. It is a great accomplishment. What you have done here can be compared to the civil rights movement in America. People there worked hard for change. Though America still struggles with the same issues, they have come a long way to improve things."

Miguel replied, "I fought over in Afganistan. Many soldiers died fighting for those people and most would do it again. When we left, though, nothing had really changed. Everything went back to the way it was. I learned that it takes time to affect change. It doesn't happen over night. People have to learn, they have to understand what is possible, and then they can work together to make change.

The people of México have learned that they can affect change and they won't forget what they know; they know hope. The people will always unite, and one day they will win. Now that they know what is possible, we will have our country back. We will have our pride back. And, we will come back home."

"Don't fool yourself. México will continue to struggle with the same issues. The change you have created isn't permanent. The government is trying protect the children for now… because of you. But, *el Norte* will continue to make demands, and she will find a way. The children will once again be made available to prostitution and organ donation. Americans are individualists. They think only of themselves. They think of their own personal comfort. They don't want to see that their choices affect others.

Real change will only come from the will of the people; the people of México and the people of America. They need to understand each other and agree on what is right and what is wrong. That will never happen, Miguel. And, because it will never happen, I will always be in business.

Here, in México, the people are desperate. They are hungry; their stomachs burn with emptiness. They seek food, water and shelter, but they also seek pride; respect. I can offer them these things. Because it is right to provide for their families, they will accept their fate even if they think that what they are doing is wrong. They become hardened and doing wrong becomes easier to live with than being hungry. The same is true in *Los Estados Unidos*. It's true across the world and throughout history.

Americans demand narcotics. They think that as long as they have the money to pay, they should be able to have what they want. As long as there is demand, someone will supply.

Your resistance is falling apart. Some of your men needed money and are working for me now. They are distributing narcotics and use the weapons that you issued to protect themselves. You are not taking care of them. You have given me an opportunity and as a businessman, I had to capitalize on it. They are grateful to me for giving them a way to provide for their families.

Think your decision through carefully. I ask you not to decide today. The resistance is falling apart. Think about what options you have and what the consequences of your decisions will be."

Miguel said, "I meet with the mayor often. He lives in fear for his life and for his sanity. I don't ever want to live like that. My decision is final."

Maximo took the phone from his pocket and dialed a number. "I'm ready." Before they could return to the house, Marcos pulled up. Miguel's gut twisted, apprehension welling up within him, as Maximo settled himself in the car. Anxiety smothered him as Maximo closed the door. His words began to haunt him; Miguel wished he could take them back. He considered saying that his decision was not final. That his bruised ego had responded to Maximo, not him.

Miguel kept his hands on the door as his mind searched for something to say. Some part of him wanted to eliminate the danger and uncertainty and shoot them both. He felt so threatened. Maximo rode away without a word. Miguel felt like a ghost standing alone in the street. He wondered if he had just squandered his last opportunity eliminate two problems—Maximo and Marcos.

17

Without a Plan

No one had much to say as Miguel updated the group about his conversation with Maximo. An oppressive gloominess filled the room. They worked together slowing cleaning up as evening set in. The house was quiet except for the sounds of water running and dishes clanking. After all the cleaning was complete, Padre and *Abuela* said they would pray and left together. Their routines at the church demanded their return. Papi said he wanted to stay and help figure out where all the day's events had left them. He needed to be with his son while they planned what would happen next. The little house could sometimes be a comfort, but at times, Pedro felt constrained. His nervous energy prevented him from sitting still in the quiet. Pedro said he needed some air and went for a drive. It was almost on schedule.

The time ticked away. There wasn't much planning happening, unfortunately. Miguel felt his thoughts came easier to him when he was outside and alone. He could always find a small voice inside him that helped him make decisions. But, this time, his voice offered him nothing. Instead, he prayed.

"Dear God. Help me. I beg you. I am lost. I don't know what to do. Send me a sign. Show me the way. I have lost control and put many people in danger. My beloved México is closing in on me, and I want to run. It is time to run if I want to live, and I do. I want to live. But, running means leaving my people without a leader. I know they will suffer because they believed in me. Send me a sign. Show me the way. Please God, help me."

Gabriella watched Miguel wandering in the yard. He appeared worried and deep in thought. When he finally settled on the garden bench, she decided to join him.

"Have you heard from Pedro?" Miguel asked.

"No." Miguel sighed and rubbed his eyes with his palms.

"He should be back by now."

"I know. I've thinking the same thing."

"Should we look for him?"

"He could be anywhere. I have tried to locate his phone, but it must be off or something. We need to stay together, especially tonight. I feel like we are no longer safe, as though we ever were.

If Maria had said yes to Marcos today, and I had agreed to be Mayor, either of those answers might have bought us some time. Maybe even a lifetime. But, I have a feeling that the period of peace we've been enjoying only happened because Maximo was executing a plan. I sense that time has run out. We need to decide what's next. I think it's time to leave for a while, possibly forever."

"I'm sorry," Gabriella said.

"What are you sorry about?"

"I really messed things up."

"No. You didn't." Miguel assured her. "Hey, we have done the best we could. Both of us. All of us. The situation is completely impossible. You tried to warn me from the start. I didn't listen. And, I don't know what to do. I am thinking we need to go deeper into México, to the South. As Mexican's, I think it will be easier to disappear in México than anywhere else. Maybe México City will protect us. I think we need to head out when Pedro comes back—tonight. Let's see what he has learned on his ride."

"Do we have to decide tonight? Do you think things will seem clearer in the morning?"

"I don't know. That scene with Marcos today kind of blew my mind. Can you believe he thought Maria would marry him at thirteen years old?

"I'm guessing you don't remember what we were doing at thirteen." Gabriella said, grinning.

"We weren't getting married. And, that was different. We were in love." Miguel watched Gabriella who had become uncharacteristically timid, studying her knees became more interesting than meeting his eyes.

"Miguel, do you think we can ever find our way back to there? To being in love?"

Miguel smiled and put his arm over her shoulder. "Why do you think I ever left there?"

"So, you're not ashamed of me?"

"No, Gabs. I am a little afraid of you, but not ashamed of you. I will admit that I am still not comfortable with so many of the choices you made, but I will also admit that if you hadn't done what you did, we probably wouldn't have gotten this far."

"That's what your *Abuela* said too."

"She's a smart lady. You've done a lot of good Gabs. You've been the backbone of this whole movement. You were never afraid and always did what needed to be done, without hesitation. You have a clear inner voice."

"You give me too much credit, Miguel. I was and still am frightened. But, I am not as fearful now that I know you are not disappointed in me."

"If I am angry at anyone, it's me. I am mad at myself and this impossible situation." Miguel admitted." I have been hoping to find my way home since I was thirteen. I lost you, my mother and brother, my house, my country and even myself the day that I left México. I can't get some of that back. My family and the years are gone forever. I thought I needed to be here in this house to feel at home. But, somehow even in the chaos we have been dealing with, I know that I will always feel at home as long as I have you, and Maria too, in my life."

"I'm glad to hear that," Gabriella sounded relieved. "I never stopped loving you either. I don't know how we are going to get out of this mess, but I know we have to do this together."

Miguel leaned down to kissed Gabriella's lips, and this time, she didn't pull away. She kissed him back.

***

There were no calls from Pedro, and he didn't return. An unsettled feeling continued to build in Miguel. He paced, wearing a path around the yard as the moonlight revived dark silhouettes upon the ground. His own shadow, which seemed to mock and threaten him as it sprang to life, mimicked his gate as he set up several trip wires around the yard area and scattered twigs and tin cans around too. He was as nervous as he had been during his first night in the house. He knew that these obstacles would only buy him a second or two, but he was not going down without a fight. Miguel waited, remembering how easy it had been for Maximo's men to snatch Frankie away in broad daylight. He worried that it might have been even easier to hunt and capture Pedro.

Once inside Miguel repeatedly whispered to the air in the room, "Where is Pedro?" Miguel sensed that Gabriella and Papi were thinking the same thing. Though neither said it out loud, their silence spoke volumes.

He repeatedly looked at his phone as though the answer might finally be found there. His mind had become struck on the thought, "Where is Pedro? We can't leave without him."

Papi was unsettled, too. He walked from window to window, checking and rechecking whichever gun had been placed there. As he passed through his bedroom he stroked the knitted blanket that lay at the end of his bed, admiring it. He pulled it off the bed, carrying it to Miguel. "Your mother knitted this," Papi said hoping to distract Miguel from his worried thoughts. "She used to talk about learning to knit from her own mother. She was taught to save the ends of every skein of yarn to use in making multicolored afghans."

"I know you are trying to help, Papi. Normally, I would appreciate the distraction, but not tonight."

"You were never interested in knitting stories back then either, as I remember it." Papi chided Miguel.

"Papi, I've made a decision. We are going to leave without Pedro if he doesn't show his face soon. I can give him another hour. Do you agree?"

"Sure," Papi answered reluctantly, sick at the thought of leaving without Pedro. Frankie's torture still plagued everyone's minds. Papi returned the blanket to the bedroom. Miguel guessed by the thuds and bangs that Papi was digging around in his closet. He re-emerged with an old Mexican guitar. "Do you remember this, my *vihuela*. I haven't seen it in years."

Miguel did remember the guitar. His interest waned immediately after remembering it though, glad only that the clamor was over. Papi sat down and patiently began to tune the old instrument. Miguel stood up and continued glancing at his watch and walking around the room. "Do you really think this is a good time to be making so much noise?" The sweet sounds of the old guitar had been preserved; time had not affected its beauty. Miguel fought the urge to listen, but as Papi slowly plucked the strings, each note began to sooth him. Notes turned into chords and chords into a song. It was barely discernible, but as sweet as honey.

Suddenly, Miguel exclaimed, "That's Mama's song. That's the lullaby I have been trying to remember. I loved that song. She hummed it all the time. Do you remember the words?"

"Let's see what I can come up with." Papi began to whisper phrases at first to himself while he played and finally he softly sang,

> *You were sent from heaven above*
> *Born though God's wonderful love*
> *How lucky could you be?*
> *Into Mama's adoring arms*
> *With innocence and precious charms*
> *How lucky could I be?*
> *My son, my son, I overflow*
> *With love for you from head to toe.*
> *How lucky could we be?*
> *In México, your fatherland*
> *A place that is so very grand*
> *The beauty you will come to know*
> *Protected, cared for, as you grow,*
> *How lucky could you be?*
> *God bless you always, my love.*
> *I will protect you always, my love.*

"I remember Mama singing those words! Finally. I was afraid I was forgetting her when I forgot her song. It's a sign. She's given us a sign. Perhaps we are going to be okay."

***

Leaving the people of his community and abandoning the resistance had never been a consideration, but now that Miguel was concerned for Gabriella and Maria, he wished he had worked out some sort of an escape plan. They had each packed a small bag and kept it with them. Heading to the South seemed like the only option on such short notice. That way he wouldn't feel like such a coward, and he wouldn't be leaving his people entirely.

An uneasy feeling that he had made a grave mistake burdened Miguel. He needed to buy himself some time. There was no plan for another attack. He had put his faith in the citizens and had felt certain that people wanted freedom badly enough that they would stop at nothing until they had earned it. He should have built in some layers; he should have been more organized. He should have recognized that President Desiderio's moratorium on violence toward Miguel could be revoked at his convenience and without warning.

"The suspense is going to kill me before anything else." Miguel said.

"Is it time to go then?" Papi asked.

"I have been thinking that if I call Maximo one last time, maybe I can take it back. I could tell him that I changed my mind, at least for tonight. Until Pedro shows up. Maybe Maximo will tell me something that will make up my mind, so we can leave."

Papi and Gabriella nodded their heads in agreement. Something had to tip the scales. Miguel dialed the number that Maximo had given him in the marketplace and told a voice to have Maximo call him as soon as possible. The line went dead. Papi, Gabriella, Maria and Miguel sat together, waiting for the return call. There was little to say. Miguel couldn't stop thinking about what Frankie had told Gabriella before he died, that the cartelistas would take Gabriella first, just to make Miguel suffer.

The phone rang and Miguel answered on the first ring. "I am reconsidering my decision, but I have two conditions."

"I am a patient man, Miguel, however, you have pushed me to the end."

"If the mayor dies of natural causes before the end of his term, or if he is able to finish his term, I will accept your invitation and campaign for the position of mayor. But, my second condition is that Maria will marry of her own choosing when she finishes college.

"Tell me, Miguel, what have you planned for when I disagree with your terms?" Miguel gave no response. "Perhaps you will send Gabriella to shoot me," he laughed into the phone. "I have a plan, Miguel. My vision is to show people that the resistance is dangerous and a fraud. The people will want my protection and my job opportunities. The rest will want my narcotics or the money they can earn by selling them. People will be happy to pay my taxes in order to be rid of you.

Tell Maria that to move my knight to E4. And, by the way, President Desiderio has asked me to send you his regards. I will see you on the late evening news, Miguel." The line went dead.

Everyone anxiously waited to hear what Maximo had said while Miguel recovered from the shock of it. He felt like a panicked animal caught in a riptide, being pulled backward and away from the safety of the shore. Forced to watch the coast, his safety, shrink away no matter how desperately he struggled, his destiny unknown. Miguel's face flushed red, his hands involuntarily clenched.

"Miguel? What happened?" Gabriella asked.

Miguel shook his head. "He said President Desiderio sends his regards. Maximo said that he was personally asked to send regards for the president."

"That can't be good. It sounds to me like your stay of execution has expired," Papi said regretfully.

"Maria, he wants you to move his knight to E4"

"Okay. But, that's a stupid move for him to make." Maria said.

"Why is it a stupid move?" Miguel questioned.

"I sacrificed a piece, now I will win in three moves."

"What piece did you sacrifice?"

"My queen."

"Oh God. It's a message. I only wish we had three moves. How long until the news is on?"

***

News report:

"For a month now, the streets of Esperanza have been turned into a war zone by a group called The Resistance. Canal de las Estrellas news team just received and authenticated the following graphic and disturbing video clips.

These clips show resistance members challenging local police, causing violent disturbances, and murdering defenseless citizens.

The group is led by twenty-six year old Miguel Garces. Señor Garces is the organizer of this rebel group as well as the man responsible for illegally providing weapons and teaching his members how to effectively terrorize.

Señor Garces is considered armed and dangerous. He has been spotted with a thirteen year old girl who was reportedly kidnapped from her murdered father's home in Esperanza. We will follow-up with more news on this story as we receive it."

The video that played behind the reporter as she spoke began with Pedro and others forcing hostages into small wooden boxes at the Gates of Hell. Then it showed Gabriella pointing a bloody knife at another hostage's neck. Pedro was then seen beating a hostage until they were bloody while they begged for him to stop. The voiceover identified Gabriella and Pedro as leaders of the crusade and claimed that they were terrorists, putting the fear of death into innocent people, forcing people to fight against the government.

Resistance members were shown pointing their weapons at police officers, others fighting in the streets, and Miguel fighting with Pedro in his own yard. Miguel saw his own angry face shouting. The viewer couldn't hear what he was saying, but they saw the furious face of the resistance leader with arms flailing and spit flying.

Two teenaged boys were shown walking into a store and then Miguel was shown dragging the two dead boys back out, dumping them into an SUV which he then drove away.

With each scene, Miguel's heart sank deeper. He remembered the boom of the gun in the marketplace, how Maximo had ignored it, and how oddly there were no other witnesses. Miguel finally understood that he had been set up. Maximo had sent those boys in to collect taxes at that moment, so that they would be sacrificed for his movie. He had never imagined that Maximo could be so clever. Miguel felt foolish and naive.

Miguel thought he couldn't watch any more when Gabriella appeared again on the screen. She was shooting the two workers in Miguel's kitchen, the two officers witnessing this with Miguel. Then she was seen crying in a rage as she explained to Miguel about Frankie, the voiceover boldly identifying Gabriella as a murderer and obviously insane. Maximo had shrewdly planned the last video to hurt Miguel the most as it showed Gabriella lying on top of her kitchen table having sex with Pedro.

Papi switched the television off as Miguel stormed out of the house to hide his grief in the darkness. Miguel wailed, directing his rage into the night sky, the sound echoing through the house. Gabriella buried her face, burning with shame, into the couch. The light drained from Maria's eyes as she began to tremble. She stared blankly at the wall as she stroked her mother's back. So many girls at the club had been cared for in the same way. Maria had not escaped her fate.

The moonlight pushed long shadows across the living room, several of which appeared to be reaching for Gabriella. Papi watched his son grieve in the yard, unable to comfort him. The end seemed to be coming fast, and he didn't know what to do. Papi searched for the tiny cameras Maximo had be using inside the house and destroyed them. Papi knew in his heart that President Desiderio's order to keep Miguel alive had expired, that none of them would be safe now. There would be no more negotiations, no more power struggles, and no more options. Papi wished Pedro would return. They needed to run.

The events of the day haunted Miguel, warping his thoughts into mangled incomplete randomness. The news report and video clips, many which had been taken with Pedro's own surveillance cameras, played over again in his mind. Maximo's move to E4, taking the queen, caused him to wince and shudder.

The familiar buzz of his phone broke the silence of the night. He reached into his pocket, surprised to see a text from someone that was not on his contact list. He read: "You have to trust me. Get what you need. It's time to go."

He texted back: "Who is this?"

"Leave through the back and meet me at the end of the road in ten minutes. You will know me then."

Miguel rushed inside, shouting. "Papi, get up! Gabriella, Maria! Get up!"

After reading the text to them, they all agreed that they didn't have much choice. They would prepare to leave, but they would decide whether to trust when they discovered the identity of the texter.

"What about Pedro?" Papi asked.

Miguel threw Gabriella a hateful stare, "I don't know. We'll have to go without him."

"Miguel, we can't leave him behind," Gabriella pleaded.

"Not another word, Gabriella. I will find him, but not right now. I have to get you and Maria away from here. Unless you want to join Frankie, we have to move."

Their bags had been packed with things like clothes, water, a bit of cash, and a passport, but they quickly added their weapons and phones. Each glanced around the house knowing that this was likely the last time they would ever see it. They reached for photos and books, but regretfully placed them back, it was crucial to take only what was absolutely necessary. Miguel decided he would leave the lights on so it looked as though they were still in the house but locked the door. Suddenly, he heard a sound in the yard. He heard footsteps land and a twig snap. Everyone froze. Their worst fears had come true. They would either die fighting or be captured and tortured. Papi was the first to move and headed to the window in the next room. Maria ducked behind the kitchen counter, away from windows. Miguel positioned himself to shoot at the door as Gabriella swung her backpack off her back, placed it on the floor and unzipped it to reclaim her packed weapon.

The first shot rang out, blasting the handle off the door. Miguel fired as the door swung open. A man fell to the floor. He fired again as another man fired back. He heard the sound of an engine as gravel scraped on the ground, more of Maximo's thugs had arrived. The sound of shots echoed all around and Miguel assumed Papi was holding his own with targets in sight. He felt a burning sensation in his shoulder as he realized his gun had fallen from his hand. He was wounded. Gabriella was still fumbling with her backpack as a man entered, weapon pointed first at Miguel and then at Gabriella. Miguel raised the uninjured hand in the air in surrender as the man stepped toward Gabriella who had stopped fumbling and begun to back away screaming. He caught her by the hair, holding the weapon to her head. Gunfire and flashes of light from the yard continued until the man stepped backwards out of the house, clutching onto Gabriella. Wearing slacks, a business shirt and gloves all colored black, he became almost invisible once he was beyond the door.

A car raced into the yard and a man stepped out as the gunfire began again. Miguel grabbed his pistol off of the floor and braced himself against the window frame which provided the clearest view of Gabriella being moved toward the waiting car. He would be forced to fire with his off-hand. If he missed his target and hit Gabriella, he risked killing her, but would save her from being tortured. He hesitated. Shooting with his off-hand meant he was as likely to hit nothing as he was to shoot the assailant or Gabriella. He would need to reload, costing him time. Gabriella screamed for Miguel. Her voice echoed in the darkness making him shutter.

Miguel was sure he would not be left alive at the end of this battle, and he was also aware that death was a better fate than what Gabriella would face. He had to shoot. He leaned hard on the window pane for support and aligned his sights. The man's head bobbed as he stepped, struggling to move Gabriella with him. Before Miguel could get his first shot off, the man abruptly fell to the ground, taking Gabriella with him. The night became still.

First to stir was Papi. He crossed the room to join Miguel. "Are you all right?"

"It's just my shoulder. Can you find Maria in the kitchen?"

"Wait. Someone is moving," Papi said. "It's Gabriella. She's getting up."

Papi looked into the yard toward the sound of footsteps running away, but he couldn't see anyone in the shadows. He heard a voice near the cars, a loud whisper. "Gabriella, come here. It's over. We have to leave here."

Miguel called out, "Who is there?"

"Quiet!" The voice snapped back. "Get out here now. We have to go."

Miguel kept his eyes on Gabriella who was slowly moving toward the voice on unsteady legs. Papi embraced Maria and collected their backpacks. Miguel watched Gabriella willingly step into the SUV guided by a dark silhouette who also climbed into the drivers seat and started the engine. Miguel joined Papi and Maria at the door. They quickly scanned the area outside and began moving toward the car. The voice called out, "Hurry up. There is no time." And they did. With no other choice, the waiting car became their only means of achieving freedom.

The window was open and Marcos said, "We are out of time. Get in quickly."

Aghast to see Marcos, Miguel managed to stammer, "Where are you taking us?

"I will explain in the car, but you have to come now. Someone escaped, so they are probably already sending more assassins. They could be on their way."

Miguel opened the back door and motioned the rest to get in. He stepped in to the passenger side and Marcos drove away, barely waiting for the door to close.

Marcos passed through backyards and fields keeping his lights out except when absolutely necessary. He seemed to know where to drive as well as if he were using streets and lights, but this was of no comfort to his passengers.

"Marcos, did you warn us? What happened?"

"Yes. I texted you. Maximo was planning to attack in a few hours, in the middle of the night when you would be exhausted and less alert. So, I had some time to get you out. But, when we watched your father destroy our cameras, Maximo became nervous that you would attempt to escape. I didn't realize how quickly he would act. His men were on their way to your father's plane, prepared to destroy it if you show up there."

"Did you shoot your own men back there?"

Marcos studied the landscape in front of him without answering. Finally, his eyes met Miguel's and Miguel knew the answer. He also understood why Marcos couldn't vocalize it.

"We wouldn't have survived that ambush without you. I know that. Thank you. I don't even know what else to say."

"Don't allow yourself to be sentimental. I did it for Maria."

Miguel turned to look back at Maria. She had been silent and brave throughout the entire day, but now she cried. Gabriella held her while she finally released the emotions of the long tiresome day.

"Sharkie has your transport ready." Marcos explained. "Pedro is there now. He will be your pilot. He knows where to fly. Shut your phones off and don't turn them back on, ever. Destroy them the first chance you get. You will need new ones when the time comes. We are almost there. Get your things ready. You will get me killed if you leave anything behind in this car."

They all began shutting down their phones when Maria noticed that she had received a text as well. Hers was also from a number she didn't recognize. It read: GET OUT. Miguel asked Marcos if he knew who had sent the message and he answered, "No. As far as I know, you have no other allies. The way Maximo has things worked out, you will be forgotten by the Mexican people, but not until they are done hating you."

"I don't understand. Why would they hate me?"

"Miguel, this has all been a charade. Everything. Those guys you kidnapped, the ones who went into the mayor's office looking for trouble, they had cameras on them. They filmed everything for this purpose."

"People didn't believe Maximo last time. They are not going to buy into his crap this time either," Miguel lashed out.

"He created doubt last time. He gave it time to grow like a watered seedling. It's bad this time. Real bad. You watched the news. Gabriella and Pedro look like terrorists. People will be horrified. There is more to come. The broadcast you saw tonight is just the beginning. Maximo has made the videos into a documentary of sorts." Marcos continued. "Weren't you surprise to see how young the boys were who went in to collect taxes? He knew they would be killed. He sent boys in so the video would be more sickening."

"I hadn't seen any of the videos until tonight. Pedro handled all the surveillance."

"Well, you should have made a point of it. You have underestimated Maximo. He made films of events that never actually happened; he used actors pretending to be killed for his movie. He has film of his own gangs, claiming that they are your men. He has footage of your meetings. Maximo's claiming that he tried to get you to be reasonable. It's pretty convincing. He basically created a documentary that portrays you as a terrorist and a traitor. He has made himself look like a good guy."

"Why would he do all this instead of just killing us?"

"You gave people hope, Miguel. And, hope proved to be so much more powerful than fear. You were winning and way too popular to quietly kill. Maximo needed to make sure the people hated you first. The people must lose hope again so that he can break them. People have to believe that the cartels are too powerful be beaten and that heroes don't exist. If he couldn't destroy the will of the people, over time, they would unite and rise up again and again in your name.

Maximo's goal was the same even if you assumed the mayor's position. He would have made you look like a fool and enjoyed watching you snap. It would serve as a reminder that the government can't be trusted. He would have deliberately driven you insane, not unlike what he is doing to Mayor Ernesto. But, he would have been eliminating any renewed faith that people had in the government while destroying you at the same time.

Marcos continued, "More is going to air in the morning. The order was given to kill you, though. It was going to look like a suicide. I don't even know what was planned for Gabriella and Maria, nor do I want to think about it. Look, you're going have to get moving."

The car halted in the darkness and they piled out into the cold night air. Miguel began loading their bags into a small plane while he thought about everything he was just told. His head was dizzy. His stomach was sick. He wondered who had warned Maria to "Get out." He spotted Pedro, already in the pilot seat and reached out, shaking his hand. "You've been busy tonight. Thank you for this."

"It wasn't me. Marcos came to me. I just followed along because as Marcos said, we don't have any other play. He really is taking a chance. It's Sharkie's plane. He says you owe him." Pedro was smiling as he said it.

"How can you be making jokes right now?"

"Look who's not being positive now." Miguel shook his head in disbelief, but realized that he was smiling too. It was a great relief to have Pedro back.

Miguel stepped outside and heard Marcos say, "Maria, I won't be able to find you. But, I will to try in a few years, when this dies down. Please, will you wait for me? Do you understand? Wait for me. I hope you make it to college. That's where I will look for you.

You're going to Australia. I will begin looking there. Be safe." He kissed her forehead and she threw her arms around him.

"I will join a chess club. Any college I go to will have to have a chess club, or I will start one. Maybe that will help you find me." Maria said as she mounted the steps of the plane.

Miguel didn't know what to say. He took Marcos hand in both of his and shook it hard, "Thank you, Marcos. I hope I will see you again one day." Marcos's phone buzzed announcing a text message which read, "It's time."

"I have to go. Your time is up. His men are on their way to your house. *Gracias a Dios* that we got you out. I have to go. Fly safe."

"Marcos, wait. Listen. I'm coming back. I won't abandon the people of Esperanza."

"You're crazy. Do you know that? You're not likely to get a second chance. Don't make yourself too easy to find. You're going to get Maria killed. And, don't come back too soon. You will need a better strategy next time. Take care of Maria."

"Wait. Come with us. What is left here for you?"

Marcos paused at the car as though he seemed to be considering it. Pedro brought the engine to life as Miguel boarded the plane.

Marcos finally shook his head no and left. Miguel watched the SUV as it sped away leaving a trail of dust in the darkness.

The runway wasn't even a runway, but more of a clearing cut through rows of vegetation. In the black of night, they could see only the beginning of the path, and the terrain was not flat. They would have to place their trust in God. Pedro struggled to get the plane in the air and just cleared a tree when he said, "That's got it. We're up. Good-bye for now, Esperanza."

Miguel whispered, "Viva México."

ABOUT THE AUTHOR

Hello. Thank you for reading Viva México. I hope you enjoyed the story. My writing resume is not extensive or impressive, so I would rather use this space to share a few other thoughts with you.

I turned my associate's degree into a bachelor's degree about ten years ago, long after I was supposed to. I want you to know that if I can do it, you can too. You can do whatever it is that you want.

Move one step in the direction of your dream and you'll take the next more easily, simply out of curiosity. All my little strides and big ones too have combined into a fairly interesting life of late. Completing this novel is a really big deal for me. I have always wanted to be a writer. I have also been traveling to places like Brazil, Aruba and Dominican Republic for kite boarding. Scary first steps on all counts but very rewarding.

So far, I only regret the things I haven't yet done and ever having wasted time. I read something on Facebook posted by Prince EA. He said, "Most people die at age twenty-five, but they show up at the grave at age seventy-five." Don't let that be you!

You will find a few pages at www.kerriwrites.com, where you can get to know the author or reach out to me with comments. I am always interested in hearing from you.

Thank you for your interest.
Warmest regards, Kerri.

CPSIA information can be obtained at www.ICGtesting.com
Printed in the USA
LVOW07s1104250216

476682LV00003B/75/P